STONE ARCH BOOKS
a capstone imprint

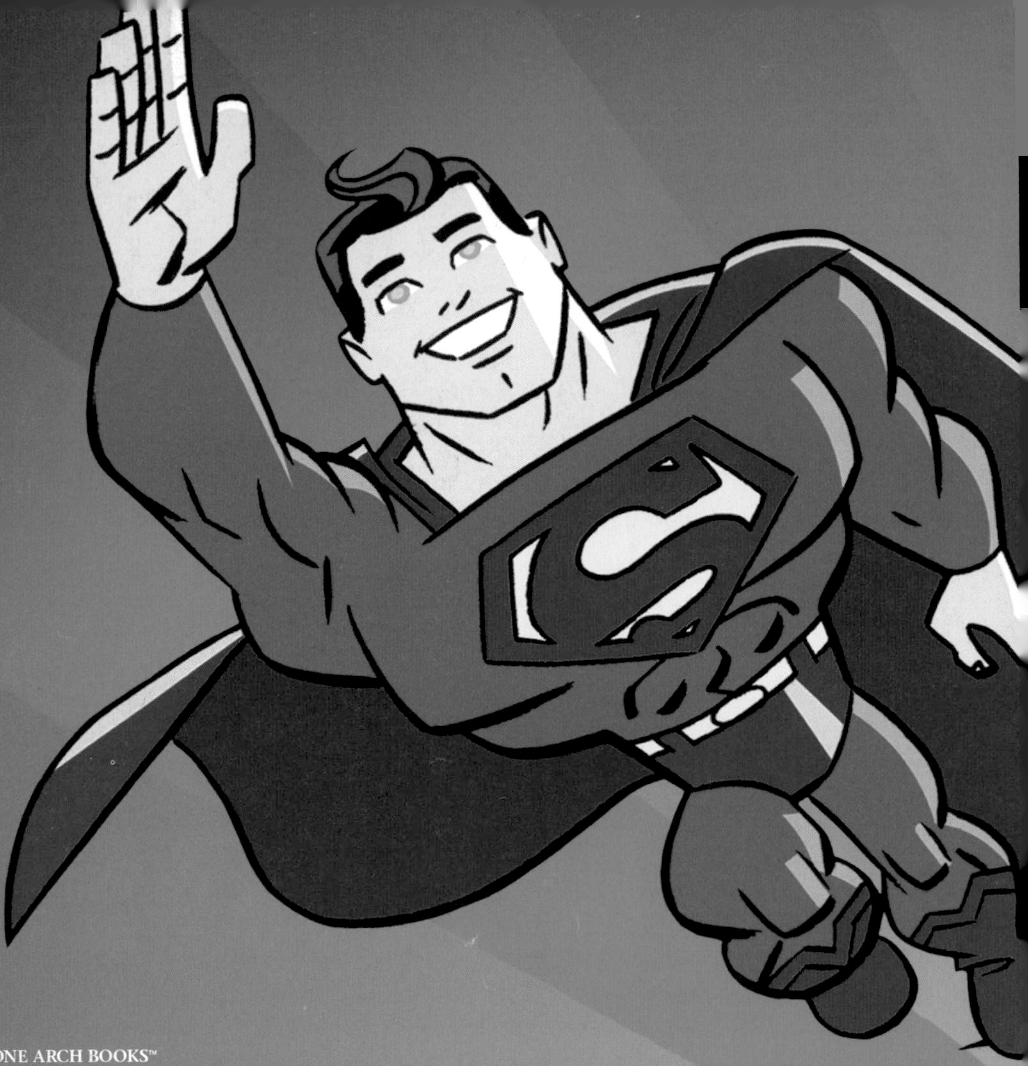

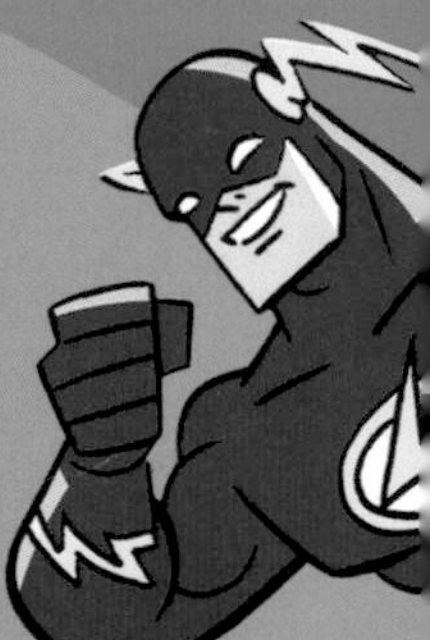

STONE ARCH BOOKS™
Published in 2012
A Capstone Imprint
1710 Roe Crest Drive
North Mankato, MN 56003
www.capstonepub.com

Originally published by DC Comics in
the U.S. in single magazine form as
DC Super Friends #4.

Cataloging-in-Publication Data is available at the
Library of Congress website:
ISBN: 978-1-4342-4544-1 (library binding)

Summary: The World's Greatest Super Heroes are
here to save the day - and be your friends, too! Follow
along as Batman, Superman, the other Super Friends
struggle against six villains secretly known as the
Jester's League of America!

STONE ARCH BOOKS
Ashley C. Andersen Zantop *Publisher*
Michael Dahl *Editorial Director*
Donald Lemke & Julie Gassman *Editors*
Heather Kindseth *Creative Director*
Brann Garvey *Designer*
Kathy McColley *Production Specialist*

DC COMICS
Rachel Gluckstern *Original U.S. Editor*

Printed in the United States of America
in Brainerd, Minnesota.
122012 007078R

DC Comics
1700 Broadway, New York, NY 10019
A Warner Bros. Entertainment Company

DC★SUPER FRIENDS

APRIL FOOLS

Sholly Fisch ....writer
Dario Brizuela..........................artist
Heroic Age .... colorist
Randy Gentile ....letter
J.Bone ....cover artist

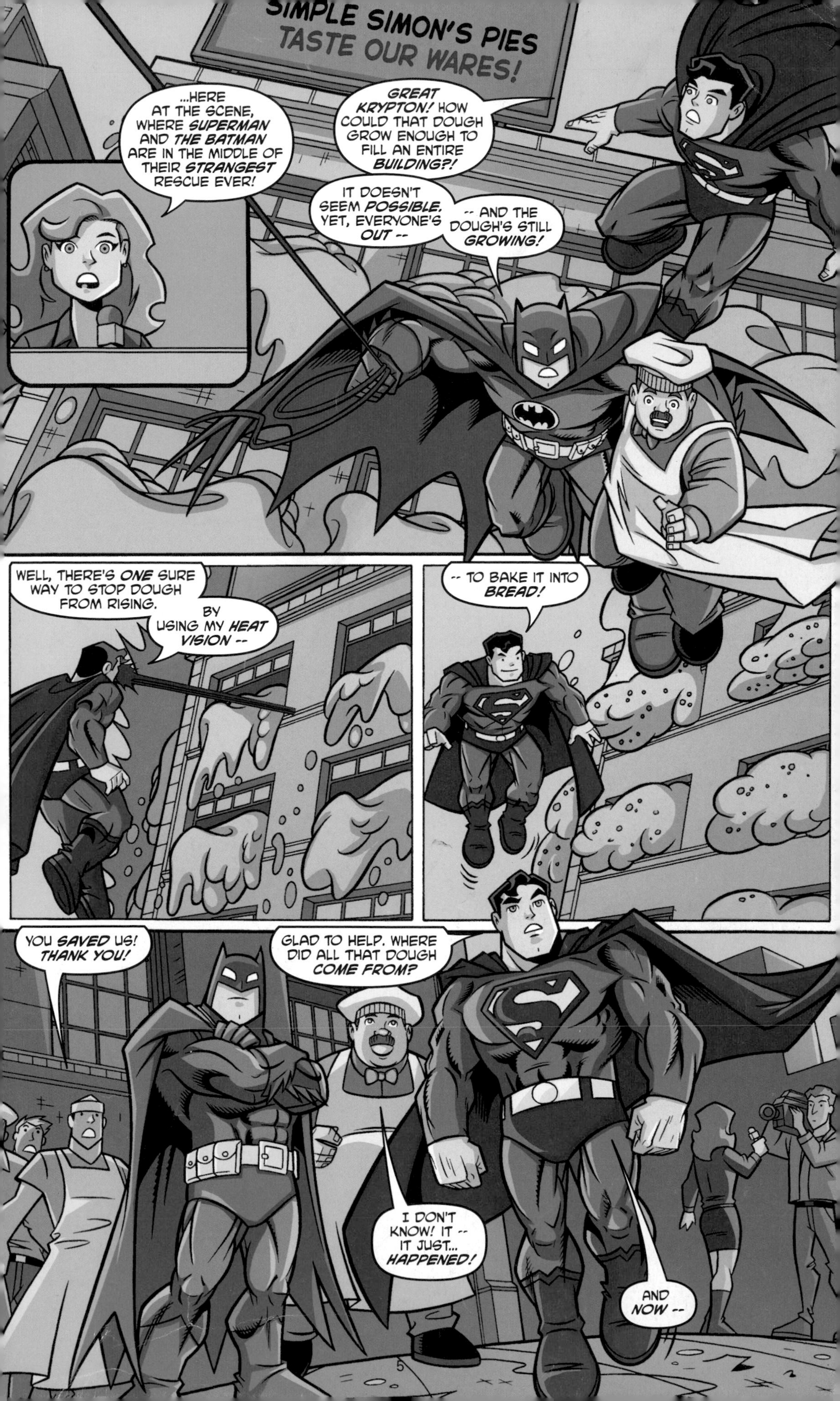
SIMPLE SIMON'S PIES
TASTE OUR WARES!
...HERE AT THE SCENE, WHERE SUPERMAN AND THE BATMAN ARE IN THE MIDDLE OF THEIR STRANGEST RESCUE EVER!
GREAT KRYPTON! HOW COULD THAT DOUGH GROW ENOUGH TO FILL AN ENTIRE BUILDING?!
IT DOESN'T SEEM POSSIBLE. YET, EVERYONE'S OUT --
-- AND THE DOUGH'S STILL GROWING!
WELL, THERE'S ONE SURE WAY TO STOP DOUGH FROM RISING.
BY USING MY HEAT VISION --
-- TO BAKE IT INTO BREAD!
YOU SAVED US! THANK YOU!
GLAD TO HELP. WHERE DID ALL THAT DOUGH COME FROM?
I DON'T KNOW! IT -- IT JUST... HAPPENED!
AND NOW --

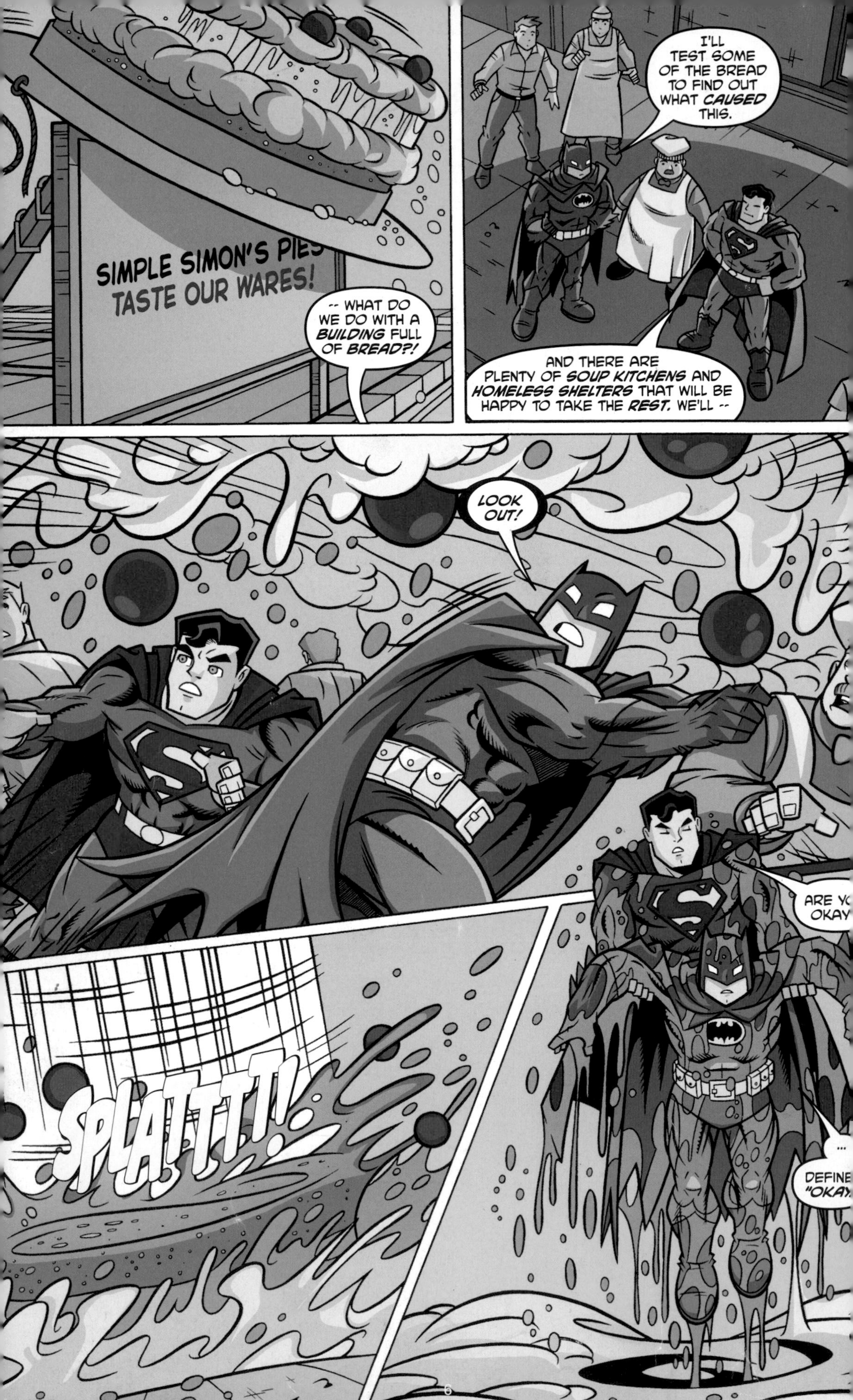
SIMPLE SIMON'S PIES
TASTE OUR WARES!
-- WHAT DO WE DO WITH A BUILDING FULL OF BREAD?!
I'LL TEST SOME OF THE BREAD TO FIND OUT WHAT CAUSED THIS.
AND THERE ARE PLENTY OF SOUP KITCHENS AND HOMELESS SHELTERS THAT WILL BE HAPPY TO TAKE THE REST. WE'LL --
LOOK OUT!
SPLATTTTT!
ARE YO OKAY
... DEFINE "OKAY

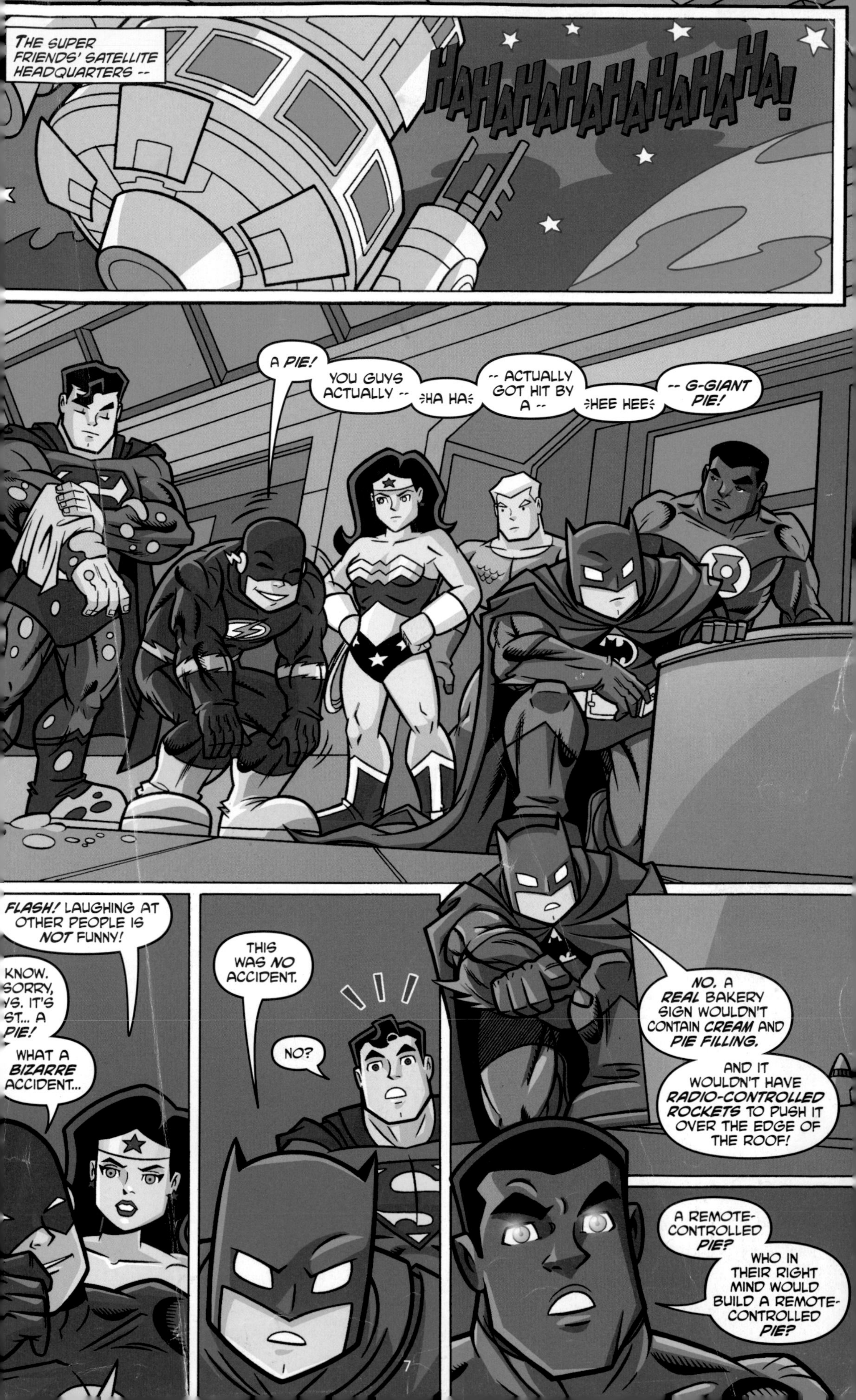

THE SUPER FRIENDS' SATELLITE HEADQUARTERS --
HAHAHAHAHAHAHAHAHA!
A PIE!
YOU GUYS ACTUALLY --
HA HA
-- ACTUALLY GOT HIT BY A --
HEE HEE
-- G-GIANT PIE!
FLASH! LAUGHING AT OTHER PEOPLE IS NOT FUNNY!
KNOW. SORRY, YS. IT'S ST... A PIE!
WHAT A BIZARRE ACCIDENT...
THIS WAS NO ACCIDENT.
NO?
NO. A REAL BAKERY SIGN WOULDN'T CONTAIN CREAM AND PIE FILLING.
AND IT WOULDN'T HAVE RADIO-CONTROLLED ROCKETS TO PUSH IT OVER THE EDGE OF THE ROOF!
A REMOTE-CONTROLLED PIE?
WHO IN THEIR RIGHT MIND WOULD BUILD A REMOTE-CONTROLLED PIE?

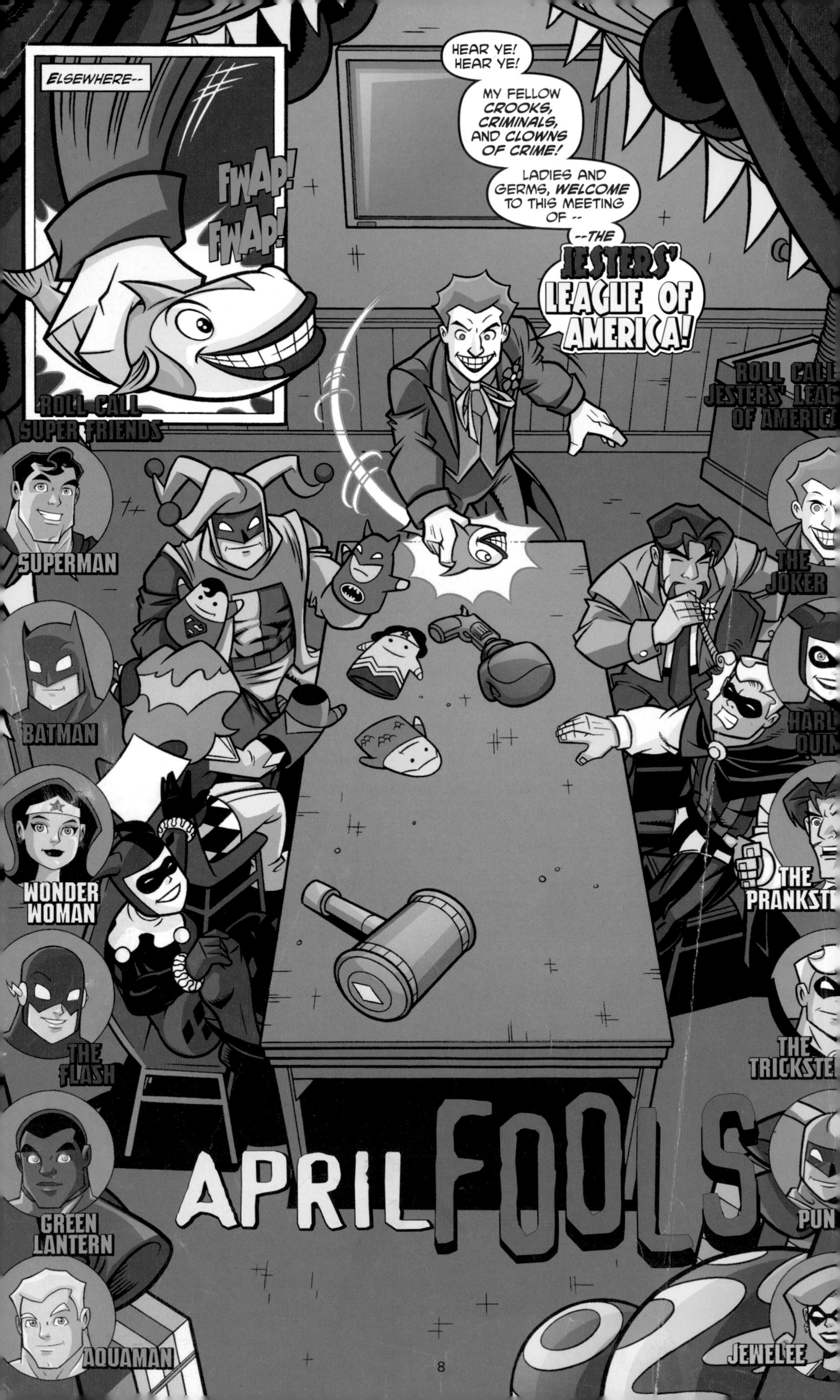
ELSEWHERE--
FWAP! FWAP!
HEAR YE! HEAR YE!
MY FELLOW CROOKS, CRIMINALS, AND CLOWNS OF CRIME!
LADIES AND GERMS, WELCOME TO THIS MEETING OF --
--THE JESTERS' LEAGUE OF AMERICA!
ROLL CALL SUPER FRIENDS
SUPERMAN
BATMAN
WONDER WOMAN
THE FLASH
GREEN LANTERN
AQUAMAN
ROLL CALL JESTERS' LEAG OF AMERIC
THE JOKER
HARL QUI
THE PRANKST
THE TRICKSTE
PUN
JEWELEE
APRIL FOOLS

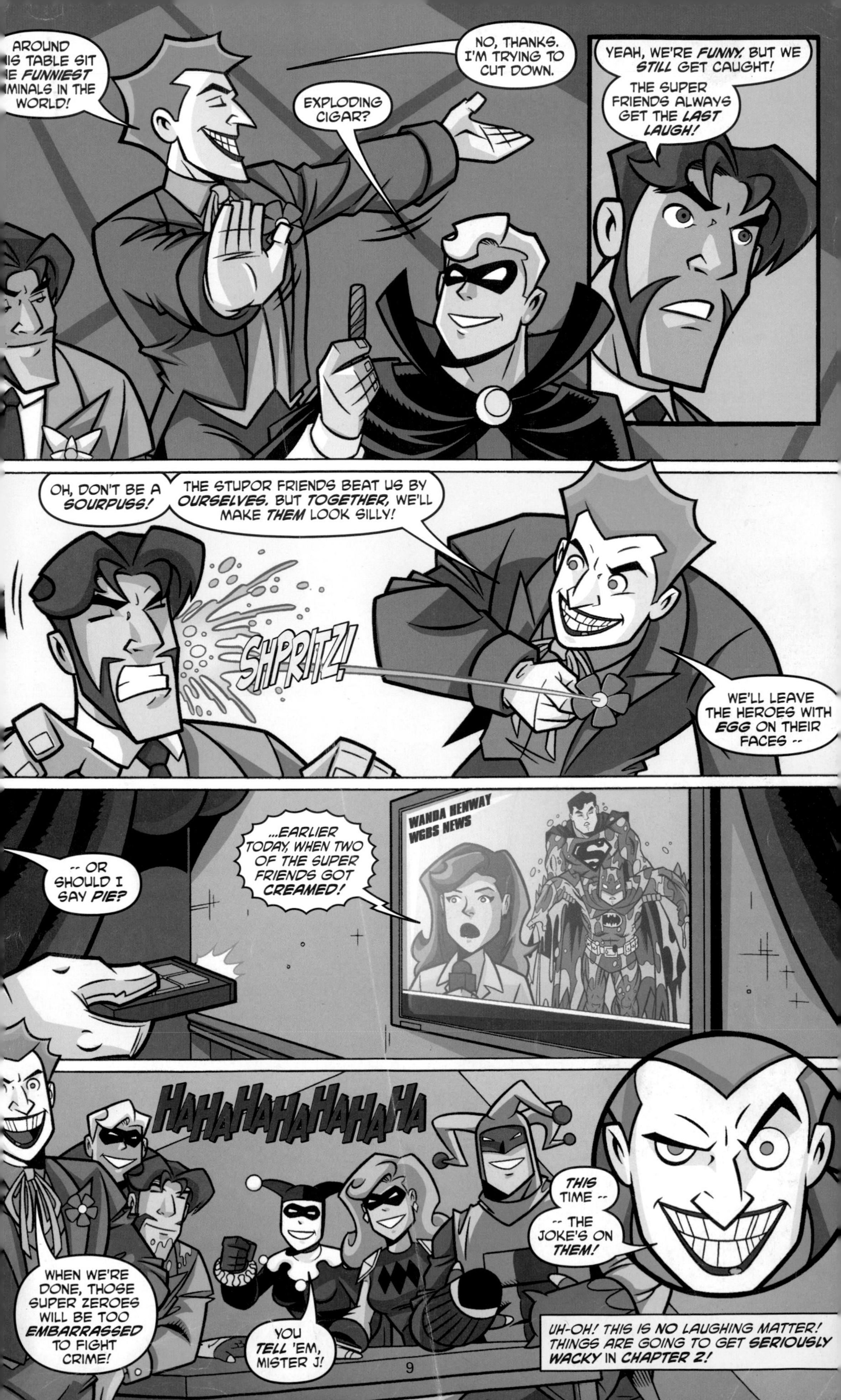

AROUND
IS TABLE SIT
E FUNNIEST
MINALS IN THE
WORLD!
EXPLODING CIGAR?
NO, THANKS. I'M TRYING TO CUT DOWN.
YEAH, WE'RE FUNNY, BUT WE STILL GET CAUGHT!
THE SUPER FRIENDS ALWAYS GET THE LAST LAUGH!
OH, DON'T BE A SOURPUSS!
THE STUPOR FRIENDS BEAT US BY OURSELVES. BUT TOGETHER, WE'LL MAKE THEM LOOK SILLY!
SHPRITZ!
WE'LL LEAVE THE HEROES WITH EGG ON THEIR FACES --
-- OR SHOULD I SAY PIE?
...EARLIER TODAY, WHEN TWO OF THE SUPER FRIENDS GOT CREAMED!
WANDA HENWAY
WGBS NEWS
HAHAHAHAHAHAHAHA
THIS TIME --
-- THE JOKE'S ON THEM!
WHEN WE'RE DONE, THOSE SUPER ZEROES WILL BE TOO EMBARRASSED TO FIGHT CRIME!
YOU TELL 'EM, MISTER J!
UH-OH! THIS IS NO LAUGHING MATTER! THINGS ARE GOING TO GET SERIOUSLY WACKY IN CHAPTER 2!

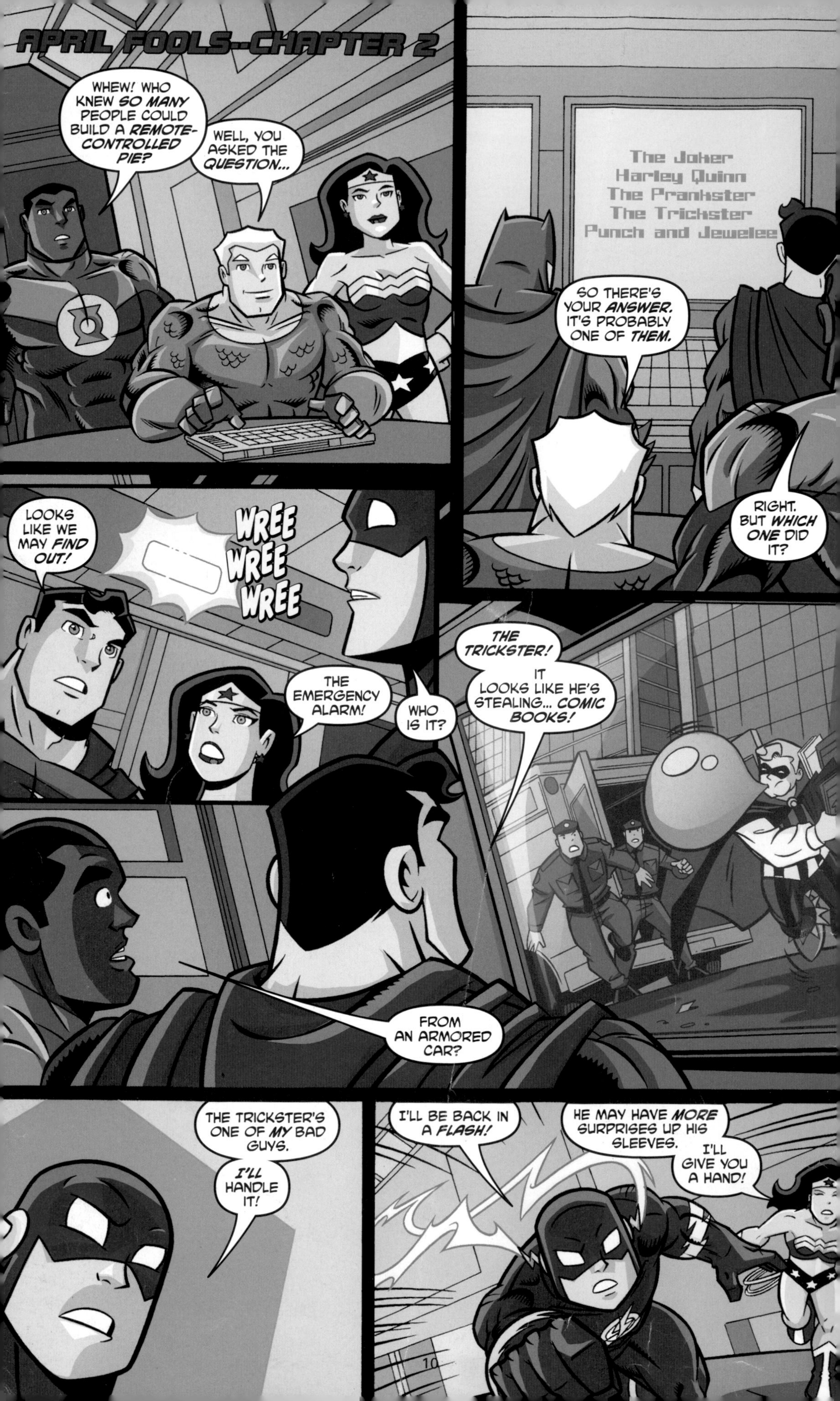
APRIL FOOLS--CHAPTER 2
WHEW! WHO KNEW SO MANY PEOPLE COULD BUILD A REMOTE-CONTROLLED PIE?
WELL, YOU ASKED THE QUESTION...
The Joker
Harley Quinn
The Prankster
The Trickster
Punch and Jewelee
SO THERE'S YOUR ANSWER. IT'S PROBABLY ONE OF THEM.
RIGHT. BUT WHICH ONE DID IT?
LOOKS LIKE WE MAY FIND OUT!
WREE WREE WREE
THE EMERGENCY ALARM!
WHO IS IT?
THE TRICKSTER!
IT LOOKS LIKE HE'S STEALING... COMIC BOOKS!
FROM AN ARMORED CAR?
THE TRICKSTER'S ONE OF MY BAD GUYS.
I'LL HANDLE IT!
I'LL BE BACK IN A FLASH!
HE MAY HAVE MORE SURPRISES UP HIS SLEEVES.
I'LL GIVE YOU A HAND!

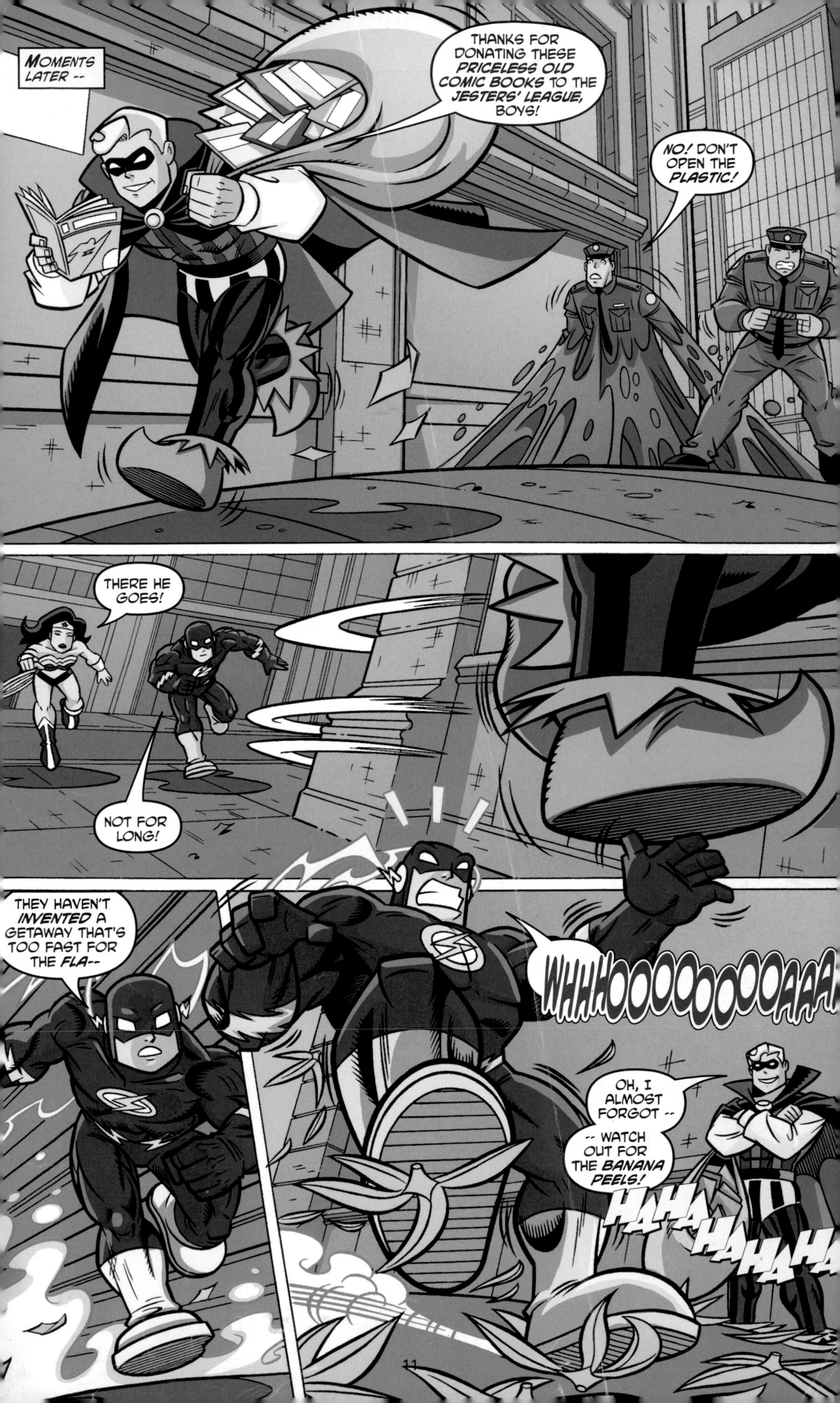
MOMENTS LATER --
THANKS FOR DONATING THESE PRICELESS OLD COMIC BOOKS TO THE JESTERS' LEAGUE, BOYS!
NO! DON'T OPEN THE PLASTIC!
THERE HE GOES!
NOT FOR LONG!
THEY HAVEN'T INVENTED A GETAWAY THAT'S TOO FAST FOR THE FLA--
WHHHOOOOOOOOAAA
OH, I ALMOST FORGOT --
-- WATCH OUT FOR THE BANANA PEELS!
HAHAHAHAHAHA

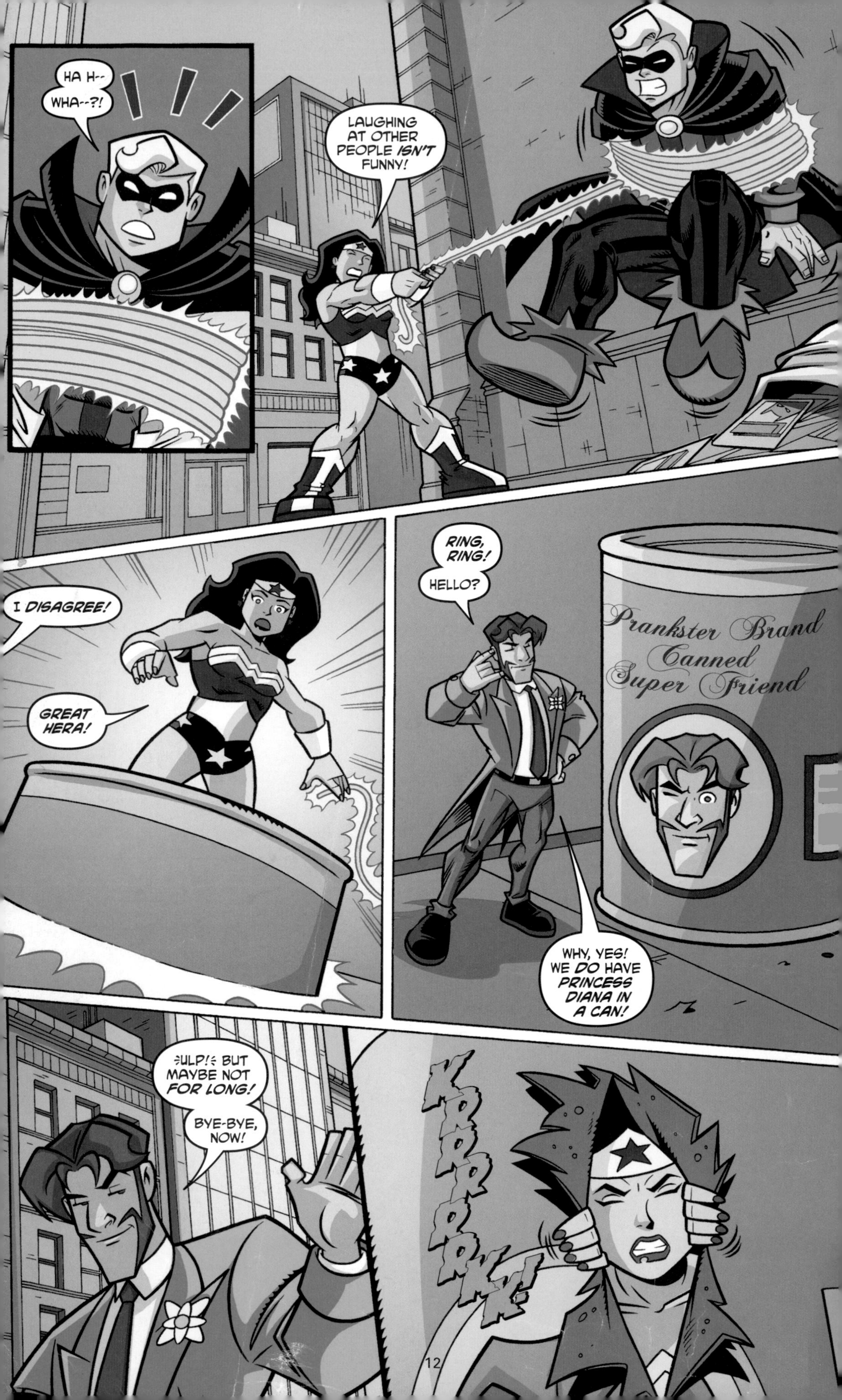
HA H--
WHA--?!
LAUGHING AT OTHER PEOPLE ISN'T FUNNY!
I DISAGREE!
GREAT HERA!
RING, RING!
HELLO?
Prankster Brand Canned Super Friend
WHY, YES! WE DO HAVE PRINCESS DIANA IN A CAN!
GULP! BUT MAYBE NOT FOR LONG!
BYE-BYE, NOW!
KRRRRNK!

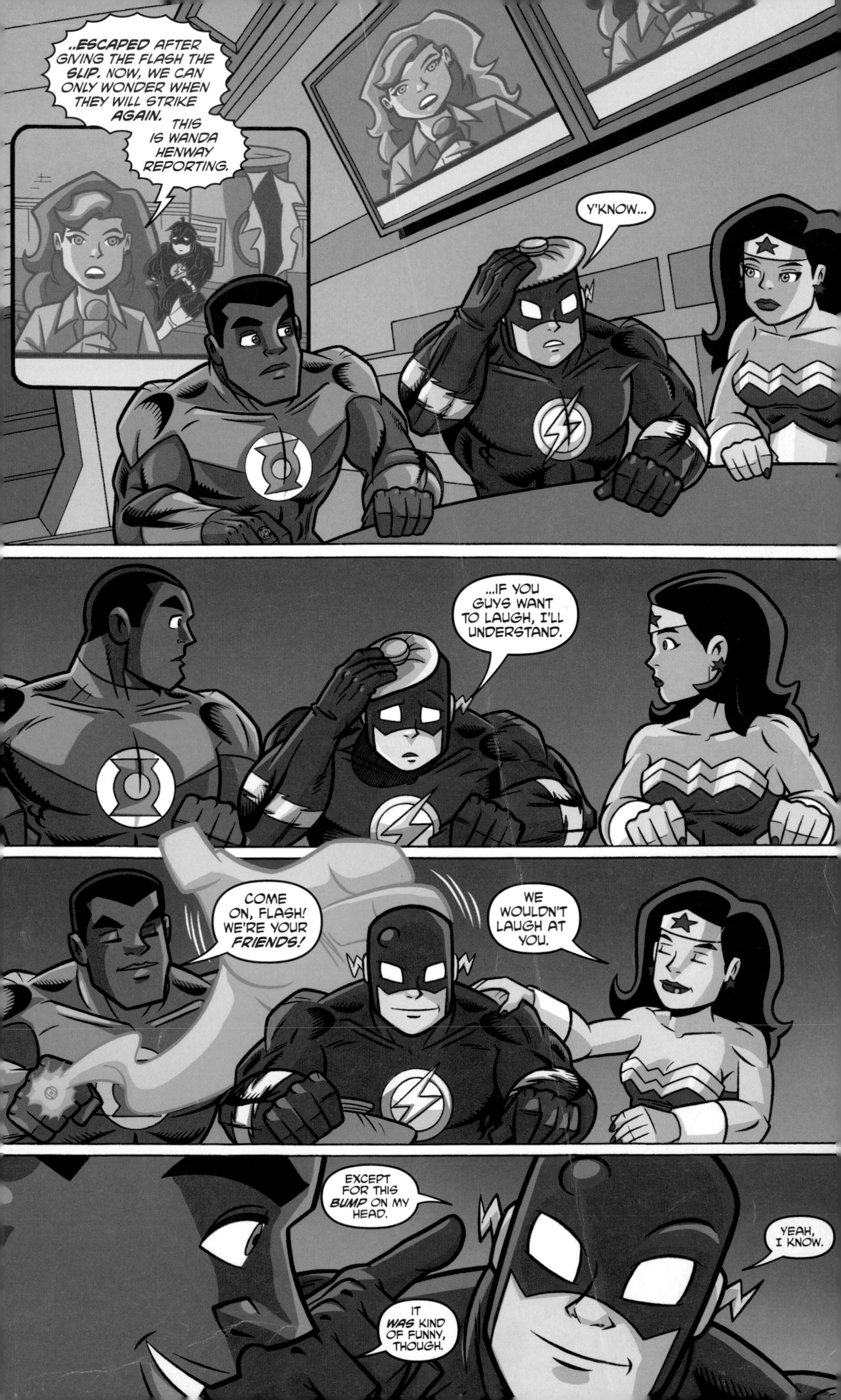
..ESCAPED AFTER GIVING THE FLASH THE SLIP. NOW, WE CAN ONLY WONDER WHEN THEY WILL STRIKE AGAIN.
THIS IS WANDA HENWAY REPORTING.
Y'KNOW...
...IF YOU GUYS WANT TO LAUGH, I'LL UNDERSTAND.
COME ON, FLASH! WE'RE YOUR FRIENDS!
WE WOULDN'T LAUGH AT YOU.
EXCEPT FOR THIS BUMP ON MY HEAD.
YEAH, I KNOW.
IT WAS KIND OF FUNNY, THOUGH.

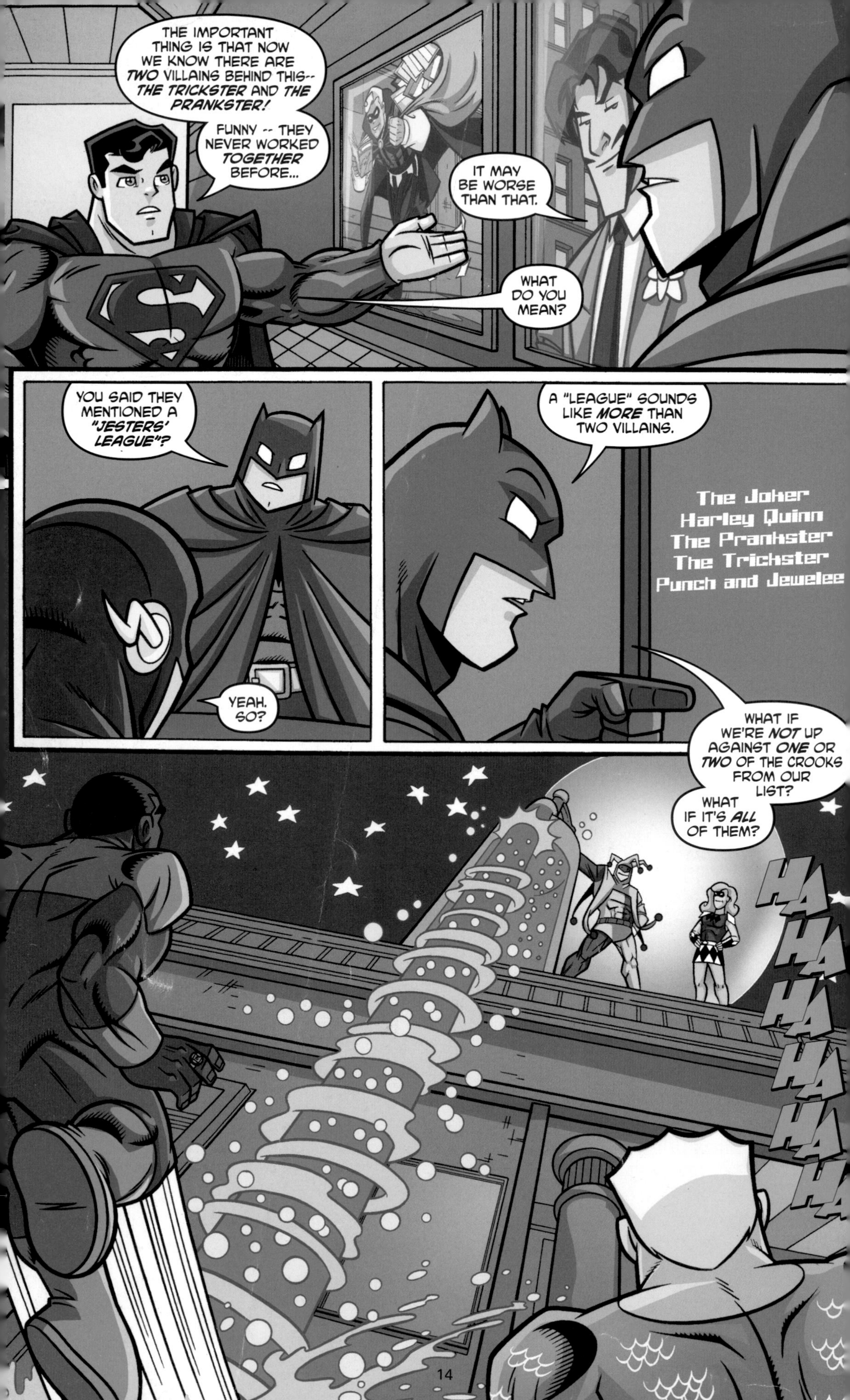
THE IMPORTANT THING IS THAT NOW WE KNOW THERE ARE TWO VILLAINS BEHIND THIS-- THE TRICKSTER AND THE PRANKSTER!
FUNNY -- THEY NEVER WORKED TOGETHER BEFORE...
IT MAY BE WORSE THAN THAT.
WHAT DO YOU MEAN?
YOU SAID THEY MENTIONED A "JESTERS' LEAGUE"?
YEAH. SO?
A "LEAGUE" SOUNDS LIKE MORE THAN TWO VILLAINS.
The Joker
Harley Quinn
The Prankster
The Trickster
Punch and Jewelee
WHAT IF WE'RE NOT UP AGAINST ONE OR TWO OF THE CROOKS FROM OUR LIST?
WHAT IF IT'S ALL OF THEM?
HAHAHAHAHAHAHAHA

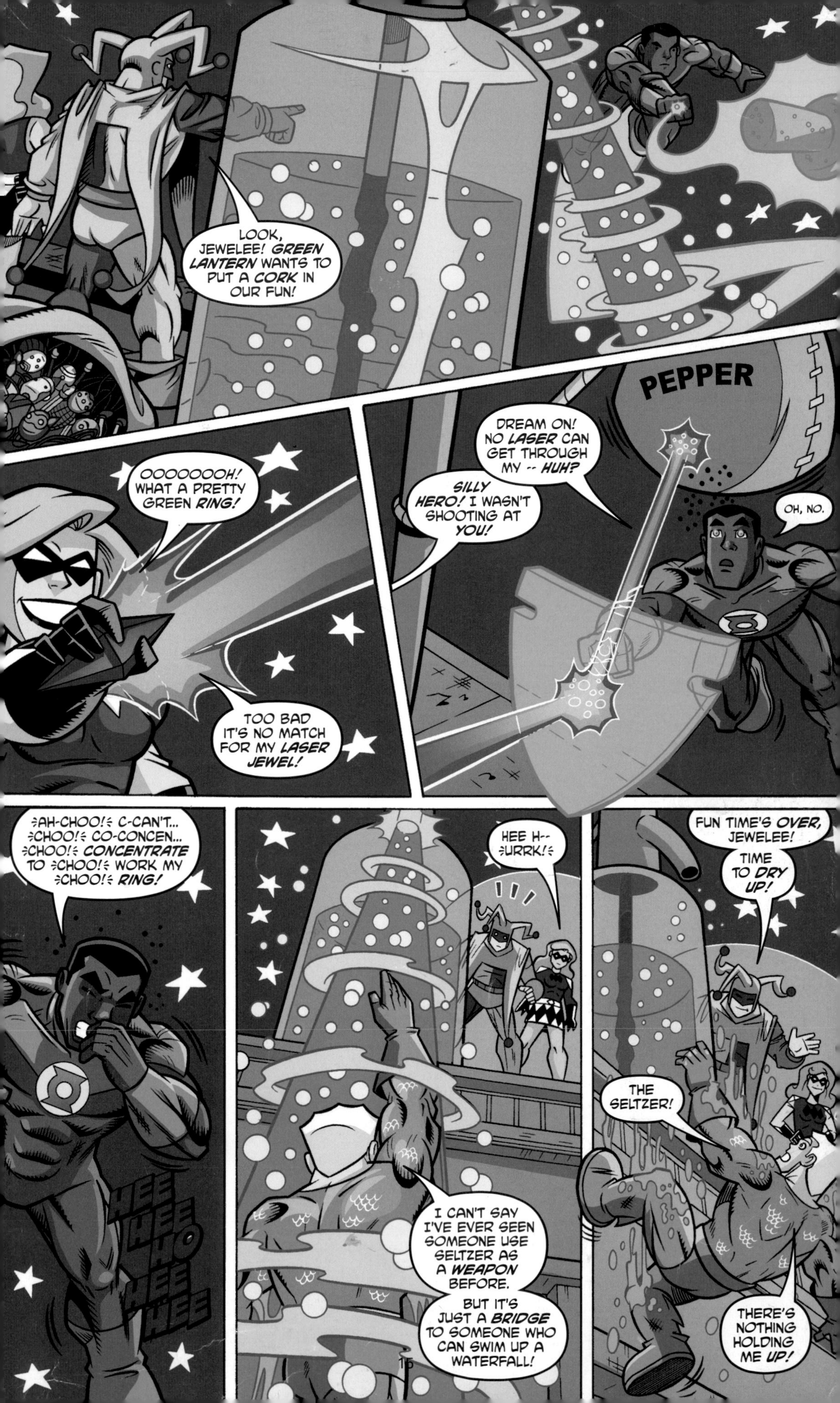

LOOK, JEWELEE! GREEN LANTERN WANTS TO PUT A CORK IN OUR FUN!
PEPPER
OOOOOOOH! WHAT A PRETTY GREEN RING!
TOO BAD IT'S NO MATCH FOR MY LASER JEWEL!
DREAM ON! NO LASER CAN GET THROUGH MY -- HUH?
SILLY HERO! I WASN'T SHOOTING AT YOU!
OH, NO.
AH-CHOO! C-CAN'T... CHOO! CO-CONCEN... CHOO! CONCENTRATE TO CHOO! WORK MY CHOO! RING!
HEE HEE HO HEE HEE
HEE H-- URRK!
I CAN'T SAY I'VE EVER SEEN SOMEONE USE SELTZER AS A WEAPON BEFORE.
BUT IT'S JUST A BRIDGE TO SOMEONE WHO CAN SWIM UP A WATERFALL!
FUN TIME'S OVER, JEWELEE!
TIME TO DRY UP!
THE SELTZER!
THERE'S NOTHING HOLDING ME UP!

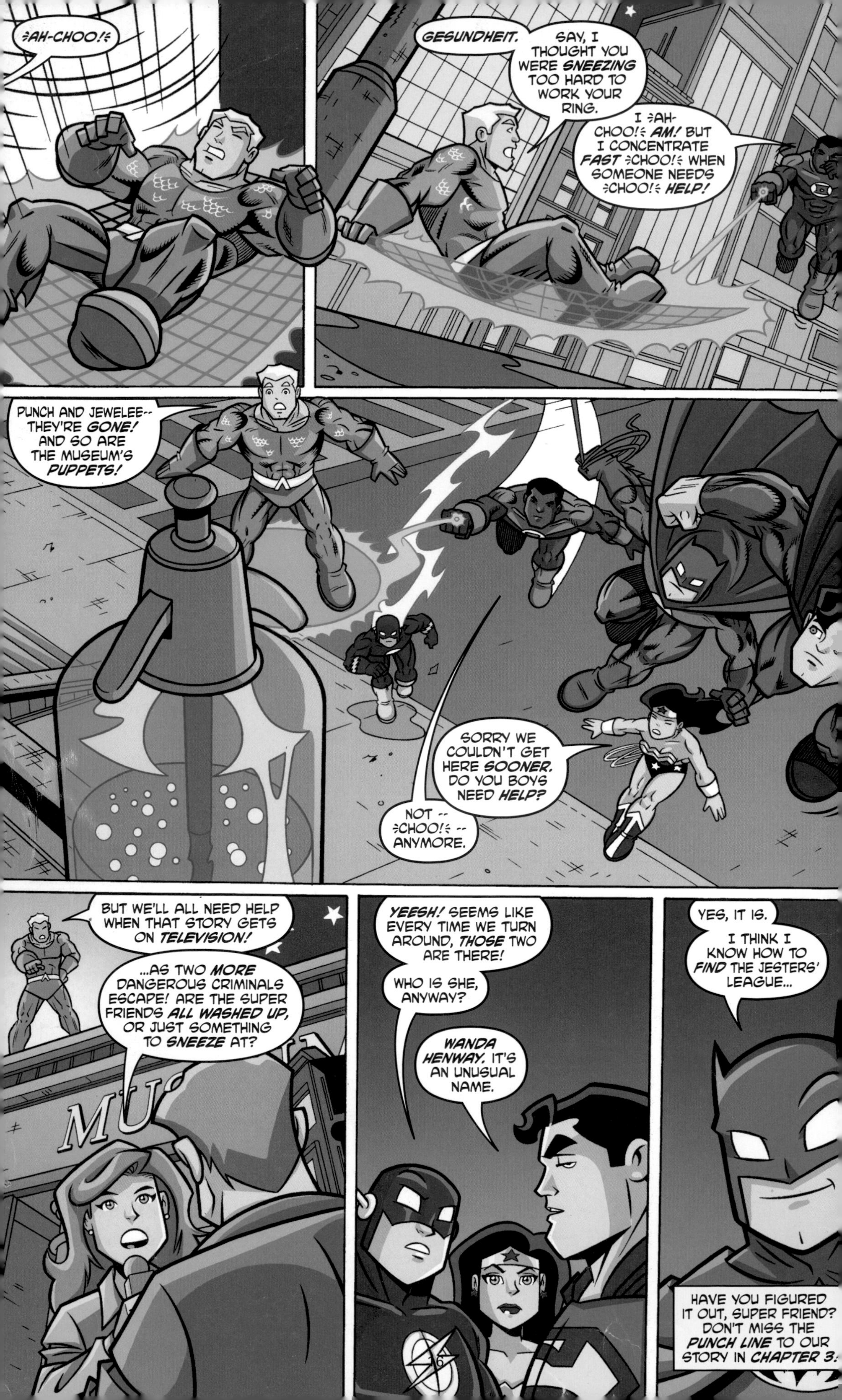
≈AH-CHOO!≈
GESUNDHEIT.
SAY, I THOUGHT YOU WERE SNEEZING TOO HARD TO WORK YOUR RING.
I ≈AH-CHOO!≈ AM! BUT I CONCENTRATE FAST ≈CHOO!≈ WHEN SOMEONE NEEDS ≈CHOO!≈ HELP!
PUNCH AND JEWELEE-- THEY'RE GONE! AND SO ARE THE MUSEUM'S PUPPETS!
SORRY WE COULDN'T GET HERE SOONER. DO YOU BOYS NEED HELP?
NOT -- ≈CHOO!≈ -- ANYMORE.
BUT WE'LL ALL NEED HELP WHEN THAT STORY GETS ON TELEVISION!
...AS TWO MORE DANGEROUS CRIMINALS ESCAPE! ARE THE SUPER FRIENDS ALL WASHED UP, OR JUST SOMETHING TO SNEEZE AT?
MU
YEESH! SEEMS LIKE EVERY TIME WE TURN AROUND, THOSE TWO ARE THERE!
WHO IS SHE, ANYWAY?
WANDA HENWAY. IT'S AN UNUSUAL NAME.
YES, IT IS.
I THINK I KNOW HOW TO FIND THE JESTERS' LEAGUE...
HAVE YOU FIGURED IT OUT, SUPER FRIEND? DON'T MISS THE PUNCH LINE TO OUR STORY IN CHAPTER 3.

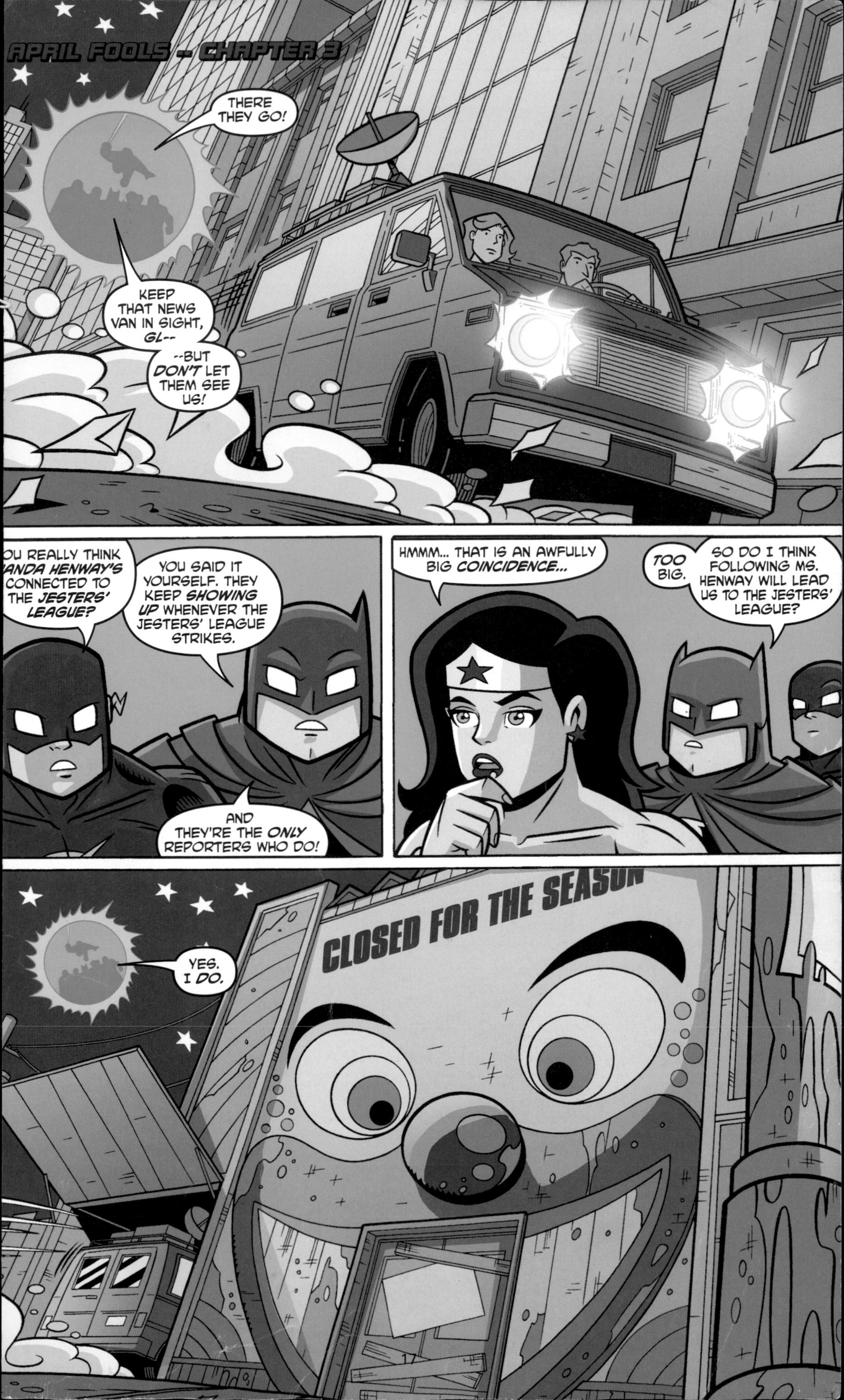

APRIL FOOLS -- CHAPTER 3
THERE THEY GO!
KEEP THAT NEWS VAN IN SIGHT, GL--
--BUT DON'T LET THEM SEE US!
OU REALLY THINK ANDA HENWAY'S CONNECTED TO THE JESTERS' LEAGUE?
YOU SAID IT YOURSELF. THEY KEEP SHOWING UP WHENEVER THE JESTERS' LEAGUE STRIKES.
AND THEY'RE THE ONLY REPORTERS WHO DO!
HMMM... THAT IS AN AWFULLY BIG COINCIDENCE...
TOO BIG.
SO DO I THINK FOLLOWING MS. HENWAY WILL LEAD US TO THE JESTERS' LEAGUE?
YES. I DO.
CLOSED FOR THE SEASON

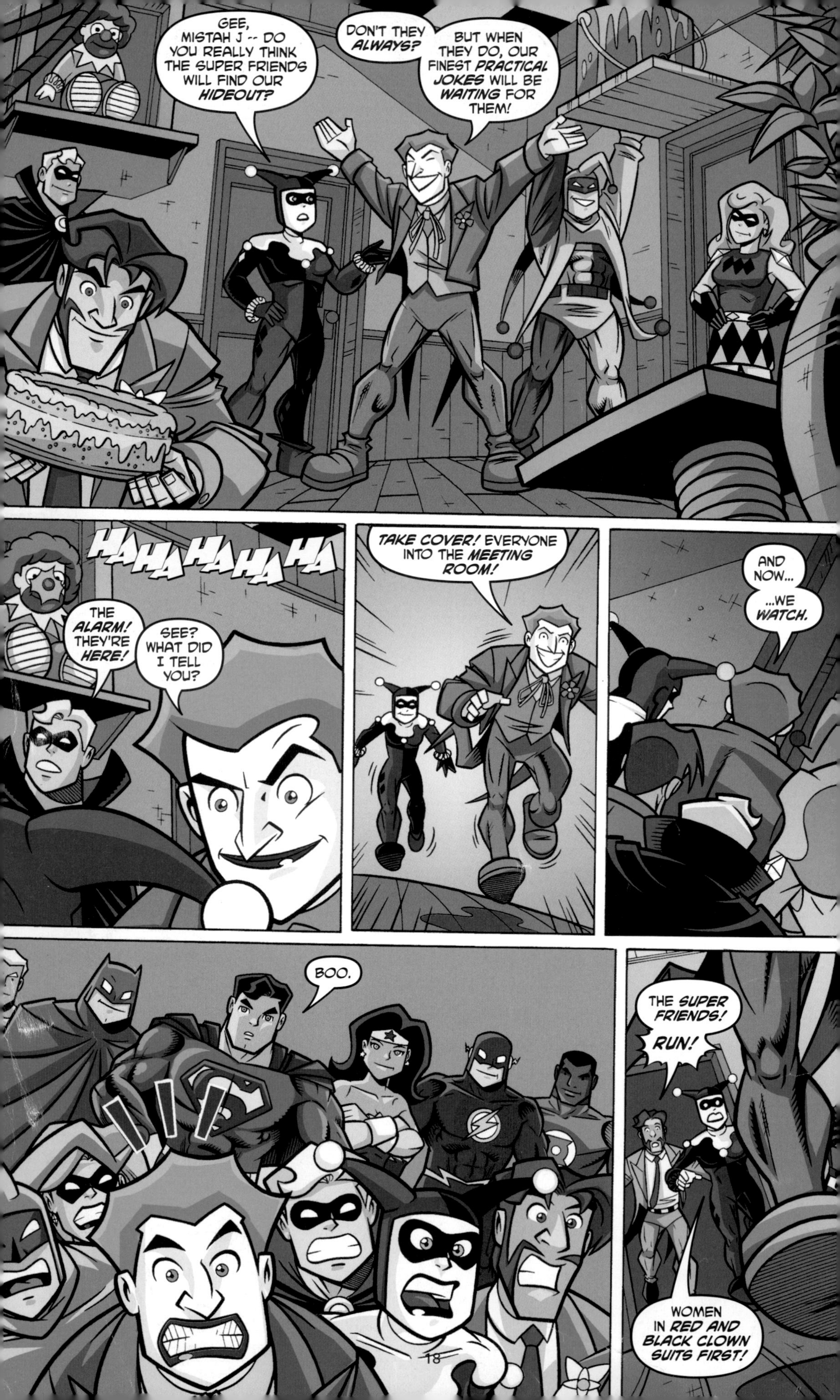

GEE, MISTAH J -- DO YOU REALLY THINK THE SUPER FRIENDS WILL FIND OUR *HIDEOUT?*
DON'T THEY *ALWAYS?*
BUT WHEN THEY DO, OUR FINEST *PRACTICAL JOKES* WILL BE *WAITING* FOR THEM!
HAHAHAHAHAHA
THE *ALARM!* THEY'RE *HERE!*
SEE? WHAT DID I TELL YOU?
TAKE COVER! EVERYONE INTO THE *MEETING ROOM!*
AND NOW...
...WE *WATCH.*
BOO.
THE *SUPER FRIENDS!*
RUN!
WOMEN IN *RED AND BLACK CLOWN SUITS FIRST!*

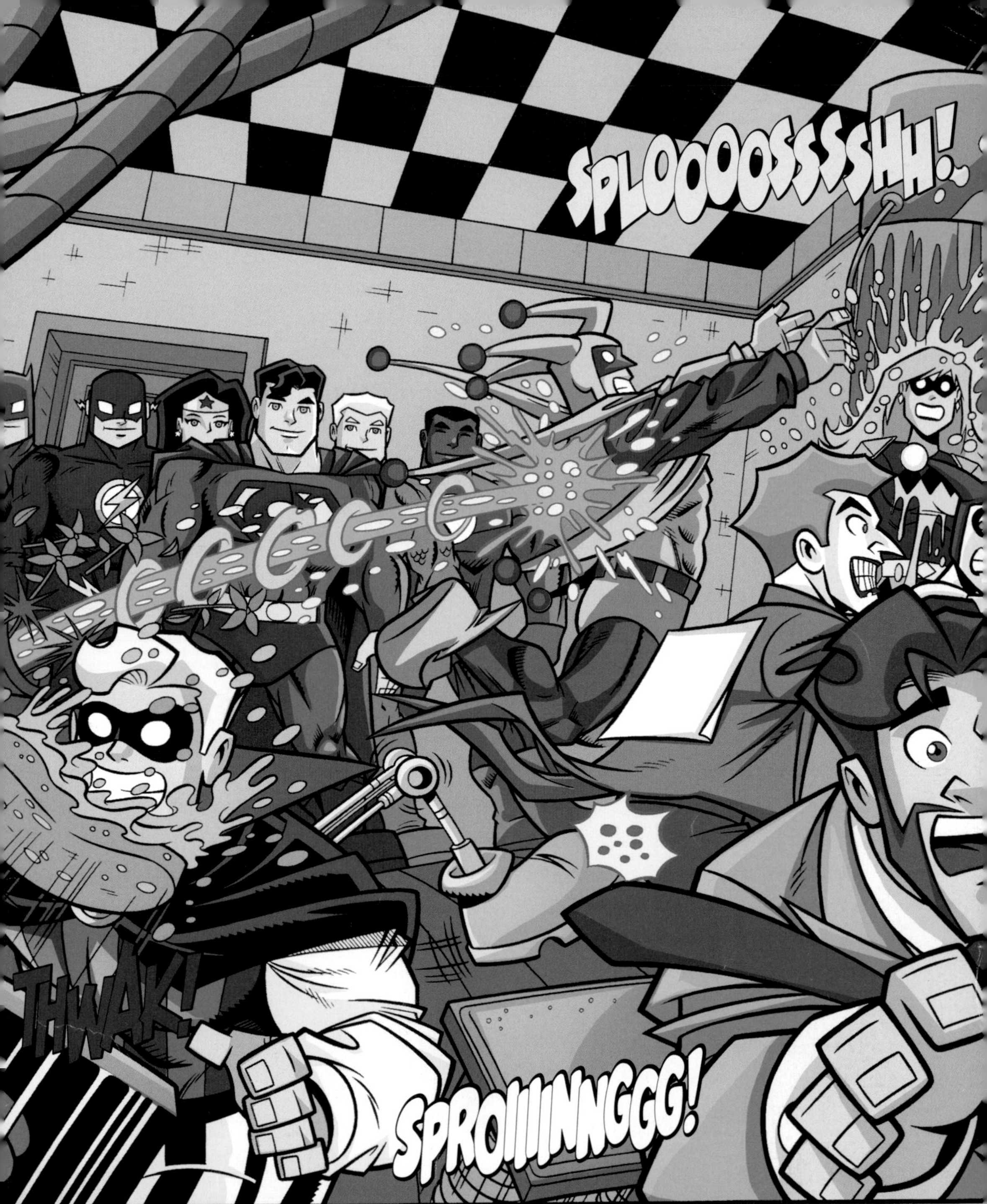
SPLOOOOSSSSHH!
THWAK!
SPROIIIINNGGG!

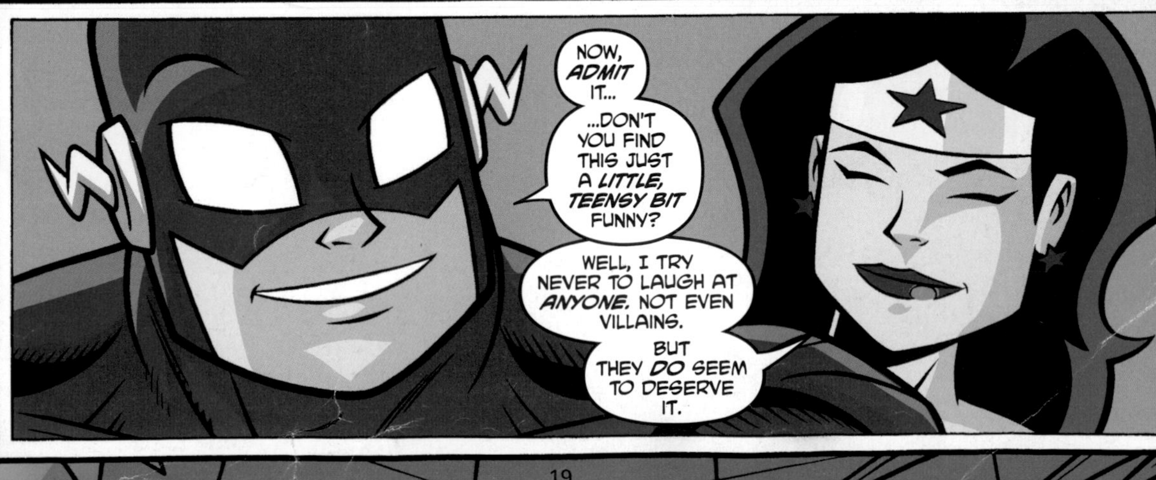
NOW, ADMIT IT...
...DON'T YOU FIND THIS JUST A LITTLE, TEENSY BIT FUNNY?
WELL, I TRY NEVER TO LAUGH AT ANYONE. NOT EVEN VILLAINS.
BUT THEY DO SEEM TO DESERVE IT.

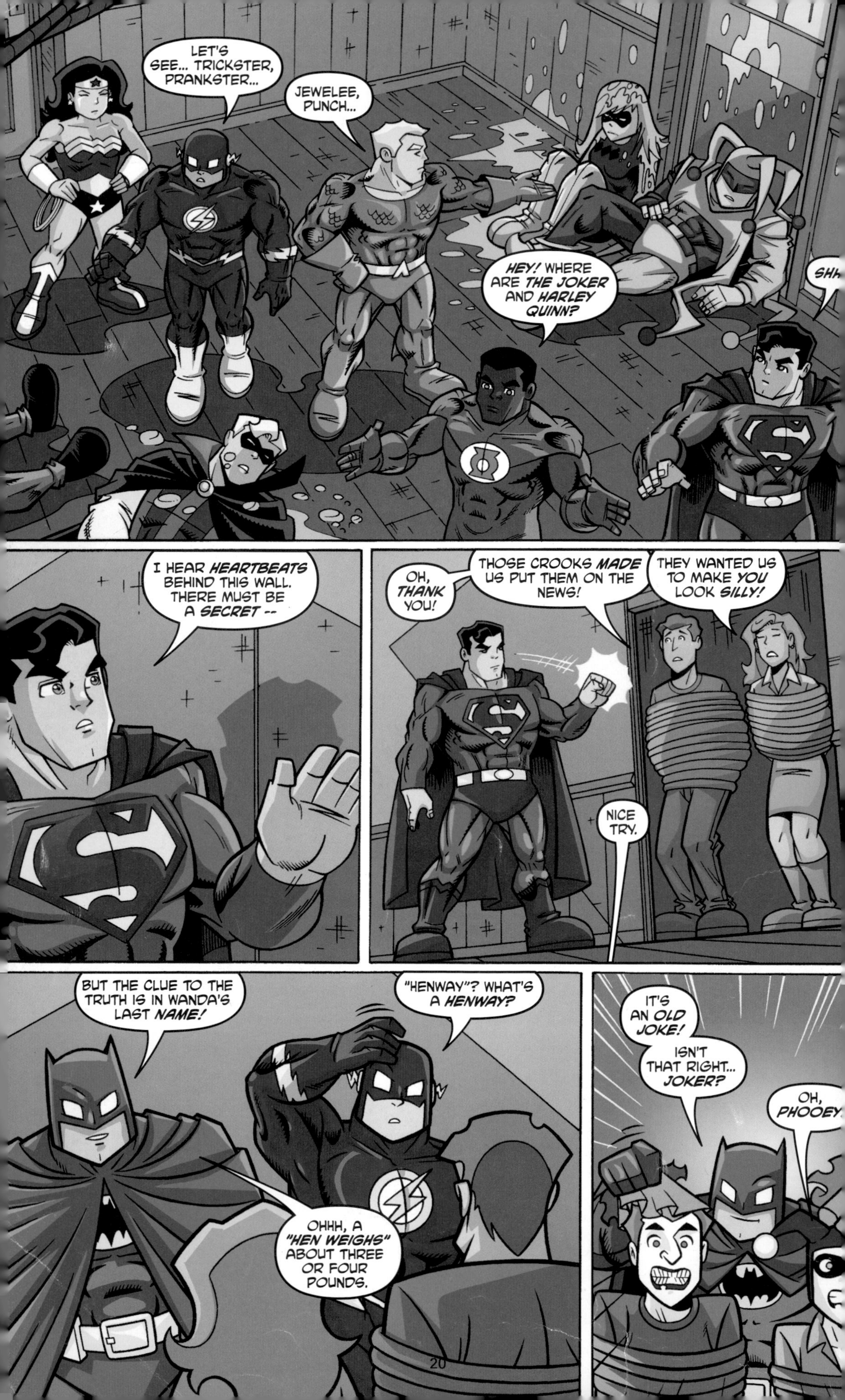
LET'S SEE... TRICKSTER, PRANKSTER...
JEWELEE, PUNCH...
HEY! WHERE ARE THE JOKER AND HARLEY QUINN?
I HEAR HEARTBEATS BEHIND THIS WALL. THERE MUST BE A SECRET --
OH, THANK YOU!
THOSE CROOKS MADE US PUT THEM ON THE NEWS!
THEY WANTED US TO MAKE YOU LOOK SILLY!
NICE TRY.
BUT THE CLUE TO THE TRUTH IS IN WANDA'S LAST NAME!
"HENWAY"? WHAT'S A HENWAY?
OHHH, A "HEN WEIGHS" ABOUT THREE OR FOUR POUNDS.
IT'S AN OLD JOKE!
ISN'T THAT RIGHT... JOKER?
OH, PHOOEY

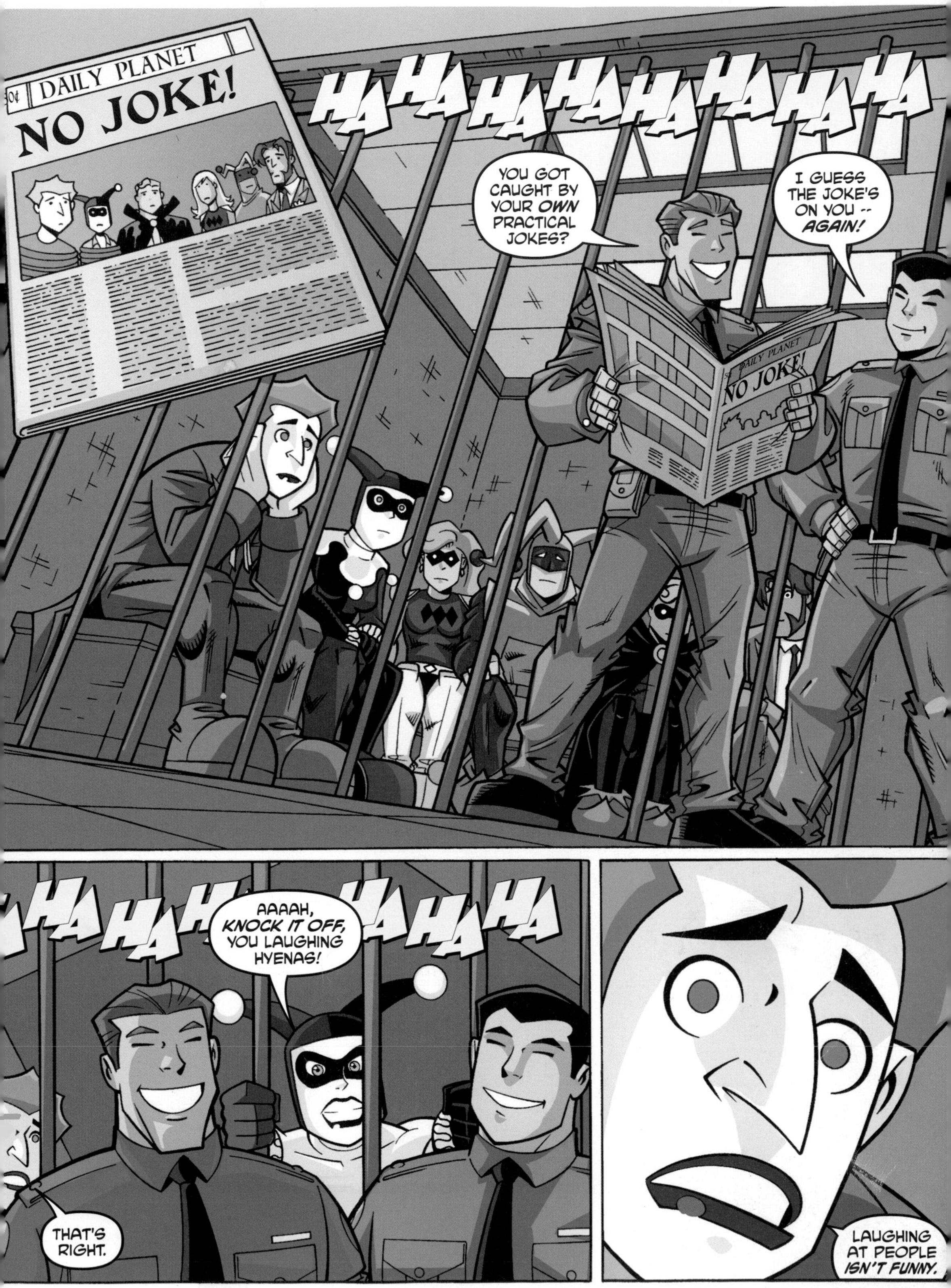
DAILY PLANET
NO JOKE!
HA HA HA HA HA HA HA HA HA HA
YOU GOT CAUGHT BY YOUR *OWN* PRACTICAL JOKES?
I GUESS THE JOKE'S ON YOU -- *AGAIN!*
DAILY PLANET
NO JOKE!
HA HA HA HA HA HA HA HA
AAAAH, *KNOCK IT OFF,* YOU LAUGHING HYENAS!
THAT'S RIGHT.
LAUGHING AT PEOPLE *ISN'T FUNNY.*

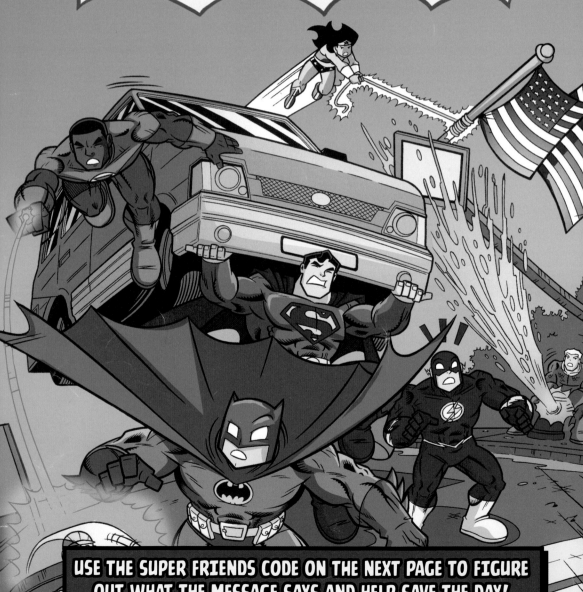

ATTENTION, ALL SUPER FRIENDS!

HERE'S THIS BOOK'S SECRET MESSAGE:

HOSXQ K PEVOY CYSOXR SP XB FBUO!

USE THE SUPER FRIENDS CODE ON THE NEXT PAGE TO FIGURE OUT WHAT THE MESSAGE SAYS AND HELP SAVE THE DAY!

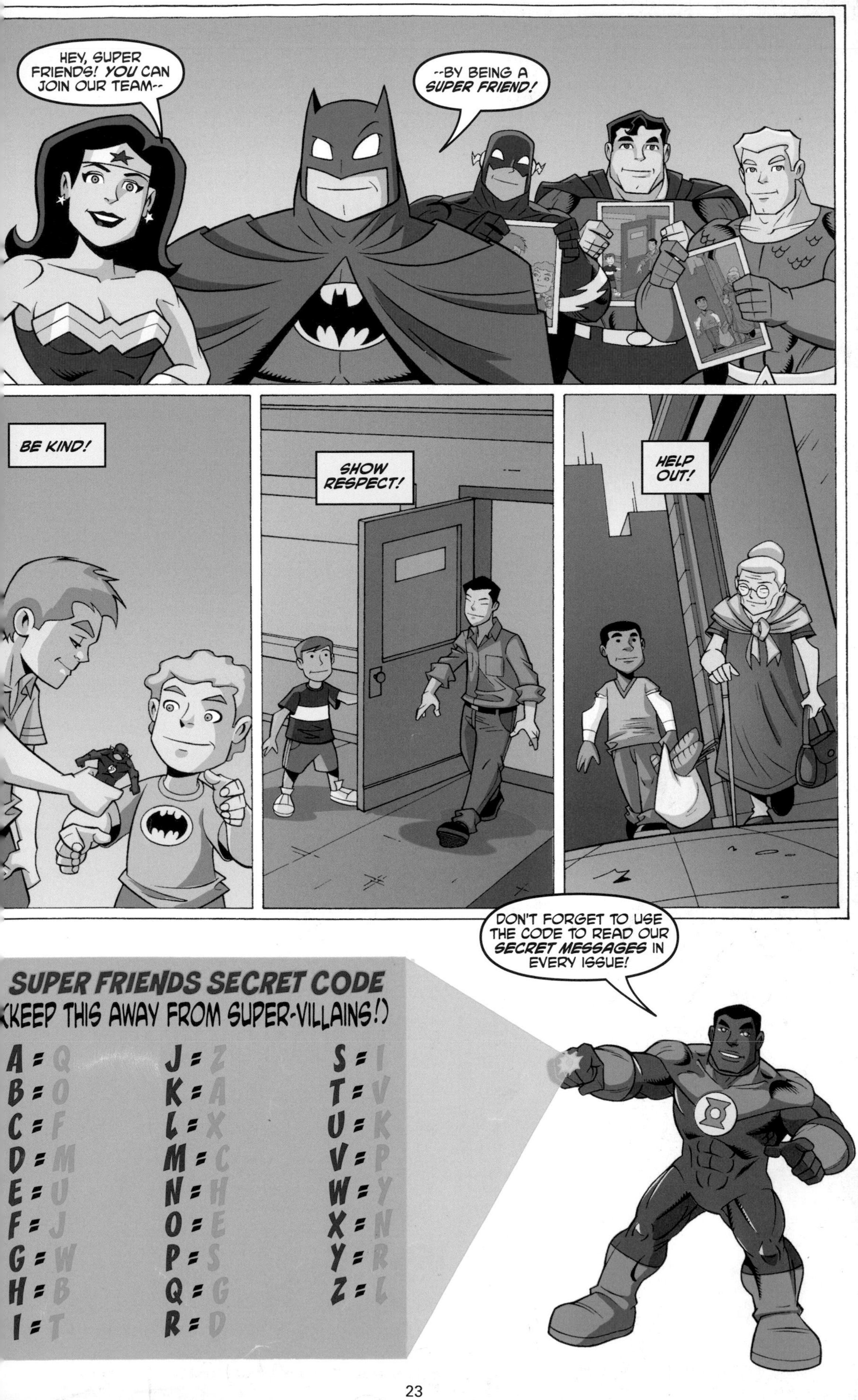
HEY, SUPER FRIENDS! YOU CAN JOIN OUR TEAM--
--BY BEING A SUPER FRIEND!
BE KIND!
SHOW RESPECT!
HELP OUT!
DON'T FORGET TO USE THE CODE TO READ OUR SECRET MESSAGES IN EVERY ISSUE!
SUPER FRIENDS SECRET CODE
(KEEP THIS AWAY FROM SUPER-VILLAINS!)
A = Q
B = O
C = F
D = M
E = U
F = J
G = W
H = B
I = T
J = Z
K = A
L = X
M = C
N = H
O = E
P = S
Q = G
R = D
S = I
T = V
U = K
V = P
W = Y
X = N
Y = R
Z = L

KNOW YOUR SUPER FRIENDS!

SUPERMAN

Real Name: Clark Kent

Powers: Super-strength, super-speed, flight, super-senses, heat vision, invulnerability, super-breath

Origin: Just before the planet Krypton exploded, baby Kal-El escaped in a rocket to Earth. On Earth, he was adopted by a kind couple named Jonathan and Martha Kent.

BATMAN

Secret Identity: Bruce Wayne

Abilities: World's greatest detective, acrobat, escape artist

Origin: Orphaned at a young age, young millionaire Bruce Wayne promised to keep all people safe from crime. After training for many years, he put on costume that would scare criminals - the costume of Batman.

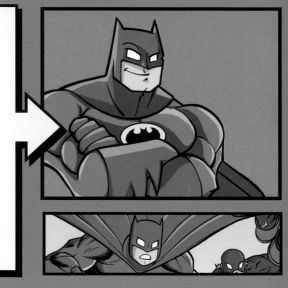

WONDER WOMAN

Secret Identity: Princess Diana

Powers: Super-strong, faster than normal humans, uses her bracelets as shields and magic lasso to make people tell the truth

Origin: Diana is the Princess of Paradise Island, the hidden home of the Amazons. When Diana was a baby, the Greek gods gave her special powers.

GREEN LANTERN

Secret Identity: John Stewart

Powers: Through the strength of willpower, Green Lantern's power ring can create anything he imagines

Origin: Led by the Guardians of the Universe, the Green Lantern Corps is an outer-space police force that keeps the whole universe safe. The Guardians chose John to protect Earth as our planet's Green Lantern.

THE FLASH

Secret Identity: Wally West

Powers: Flash uses his super-speed in many ways: he can run across water or up the side of a building, spin around to make a tornado, or vibrate his body to walk right through a wall

Origin: As a boy, Wally West became the super-fast Kid Flash when lightning hit a rack of chemicals that spilled on him. Today, he helps others as the Flash.

AQUAMAN

Real Name: King Orin or Arthur Curry

Powers: Breathes underwater, communicates with fish, swims at high speed, stronger than normal humans

Origin: Orin's father was a lighthouse keeper and his mother was a mermaid from the undersea land of Atlantis. As Orin grew up, he learned that he could live on land and underwater. He decided to use his powers to keep the seven seas safe as Aquaman.

CREATORS

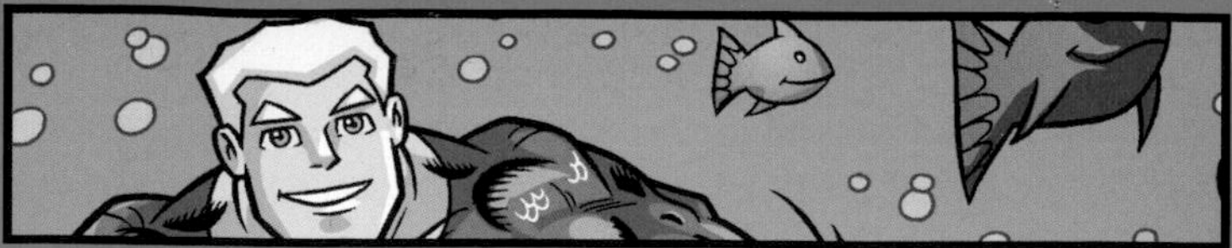

SHOLLY FISCH WRITER

Bitten by a radioactive typewriter, Sholly Fisch has spent the wee hours writing books, comics, TV scripts, and online material for more than 25 years. His comic book credits include more than 200 stories and features about characters such as Batman, Superman, Bugs Bunny, Daffy Duck, Spider-Man, and Ben 10. Currently, he writes stories for Action Comics every month, plus stories for Looney Tunes and Scooby-Doo. By day, Sholly is a mild-mannered developmental psychologist who helps to create educational TV shows, web sites, and other media for kids.

DARIO BRIZUELA ARTIST

Dario Brizuela is a professional comic book artist. He's illustrated some of today's most popular characters, including Batman, Green Lantern, Teenage Mutant Ninja Turtles, Thor, Iron Man, and Transformers. His best-known works for DC Comics include the series DC Super Friends, Justice League Unlimited, and Batman: The Brave and the Bold.

J. BONE COVER ARTIST

J.Bone is a Toronto based illustrator and comic book artist. Besides DC Super Friends, he has worked on comic books such as Spiderman: Tangled Web, Mr. Gum, Gotham Girls, and Madman Adventures. He is also the co-creator of the Alison Dare comic book series.

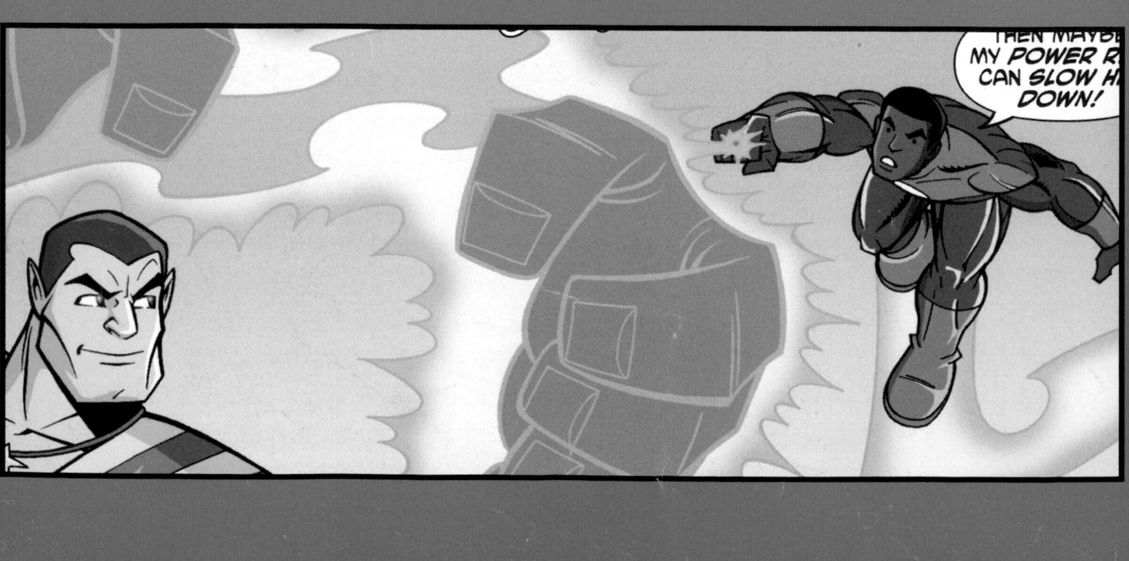
MY POWER R
CAN SLOW H
DOWN!

GLOSSARY

armored car [AR·murd KAR]–a vehicle with a strong metal covering used for moving money and other valuable things

coincidence [koh·IN·si·duhnss]–a chance happening or meeting

concentrate [KON·suhn·trate]–to focus your thoughts and attention on something

dangerous [DAYN·jur·uhss]–unsafe or risky

embarrassed [em·BA·ruhssd]–made you feel awkward or uncomfortable

gesundheit [guh·ZOONT·hite]–a wish of good health, especially to a person who has just sneezed

hyenas [hye·EE·nuhs]–wild animals that look somewhat like a dog. They eat meat and have a shrieking howl.

satellite [SAT·uh·lite]–a spacecraft that is sent into orbit around the Earth, the moon, or another heavenly body

seltzer [SELT·ser]–a type of water that is carbonated so that it bubbles

soup kitchen [SOOP KICH·uhn]–a place where food, usually soup, is served at little or no charge to the needy

stupor [STOO·per]–a state of dullness or lack of interest

universe [YOO·nuh·vurss]–the Earth, the planets, the stars, and all things that exist in space

villains [VIL·uhns]–wicked people, often evil characters in a story

weapon [WEP·uhns]–something that can be used in a fight to attack or defend, such as a sword, gun, knife, or bomb

I AM PROGRAMMED TO USE *ALL* OF THE SUPE FRIENDS' ABILITIES. WOND WOMAN'S *STRENGTH,* BATMAN'S *AGILITY*--

VISUAL QUESTIONS & PROMPTS

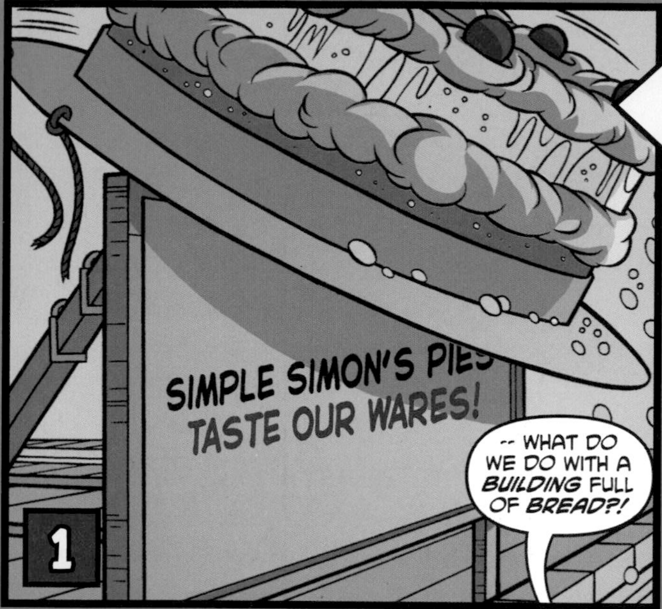
SIMPLE SIMON'S PIE
TASTE OUR WARES!
-- WHAT DO WE DO WITH A *BUILDING* FULL OF *BREAD?!*
1

1. There are visual clues of what is to come in this panel of the pie company's sign. What are the clues?

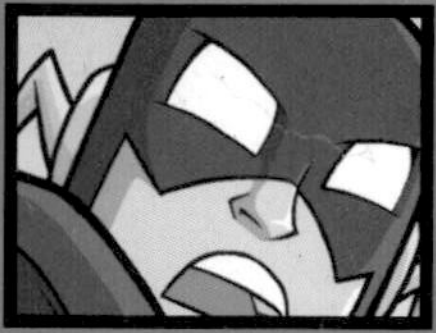

2. How is Superman feeling in the panel at right? How do we know?

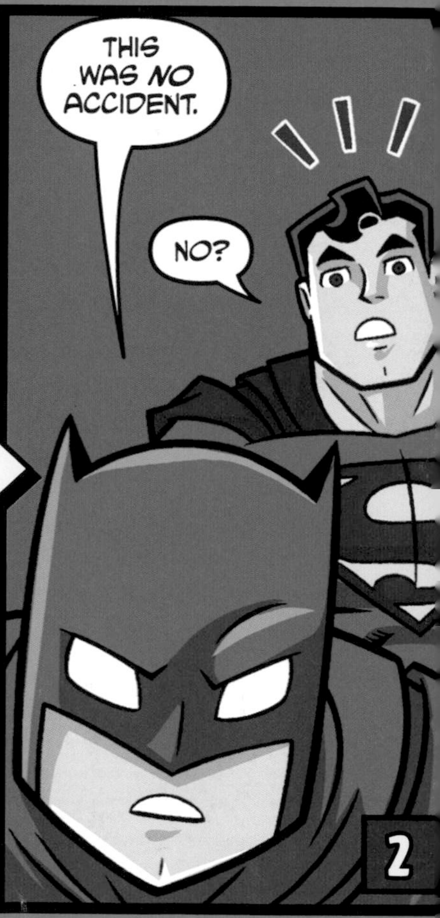
THIS WAS *NO* ACCIDENT.
NO?
2

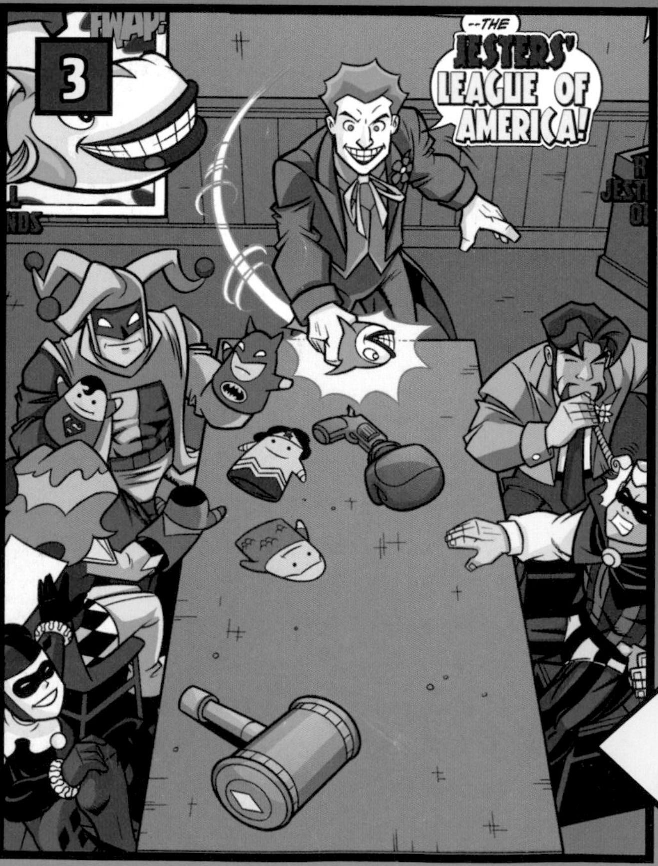
3
--THE JESTERS' LEAGUE OF AMERICA!

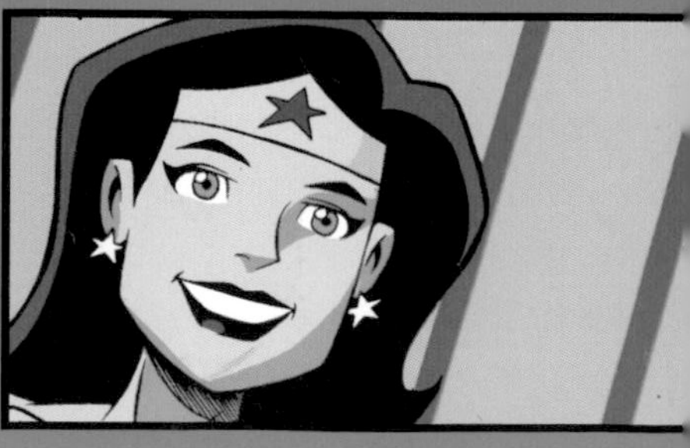

3. Practice writing dialogue for the characters in this panel. Remember that these characters are jokesters and pranksters.

4. Explain how the Trickster trapped the police officers.

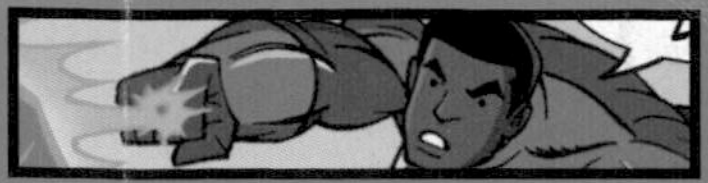

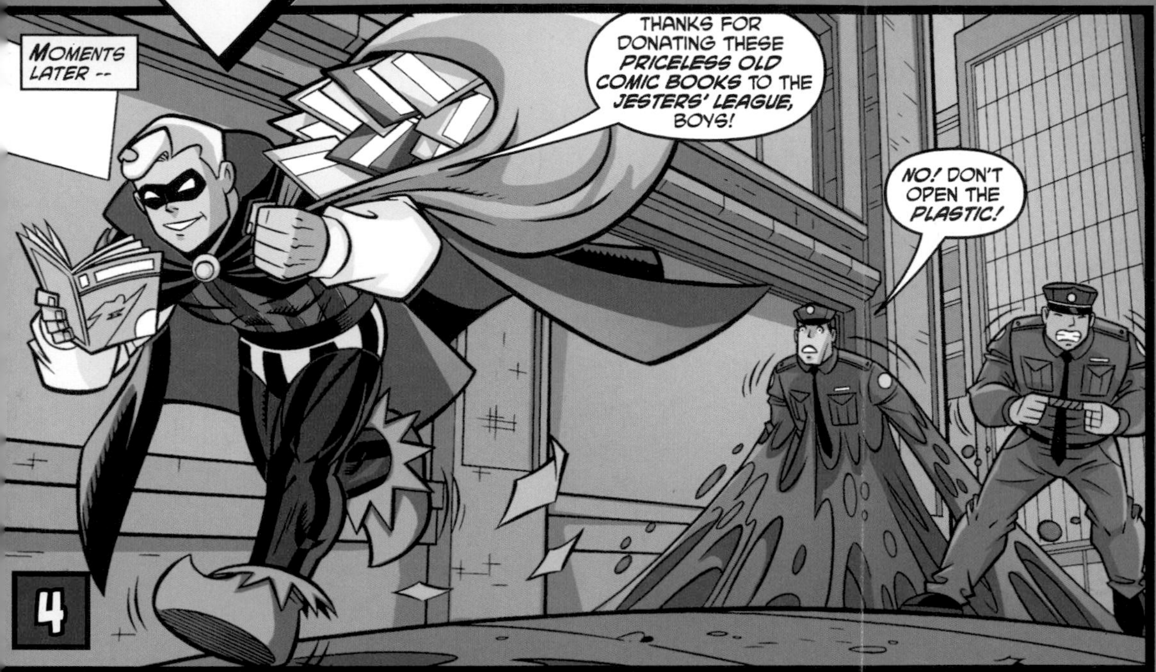

MOMENTS LATER --
THANKS FOR DONATING THESE PRICELESS OLD COMIC BOOKS TO THE JESTERS' LEAGUE, BOYS!
NO! DON'T OPEN THE PLASTIC!
4

5. The Super Friends are following the news van. How are they travelling? How do you know?

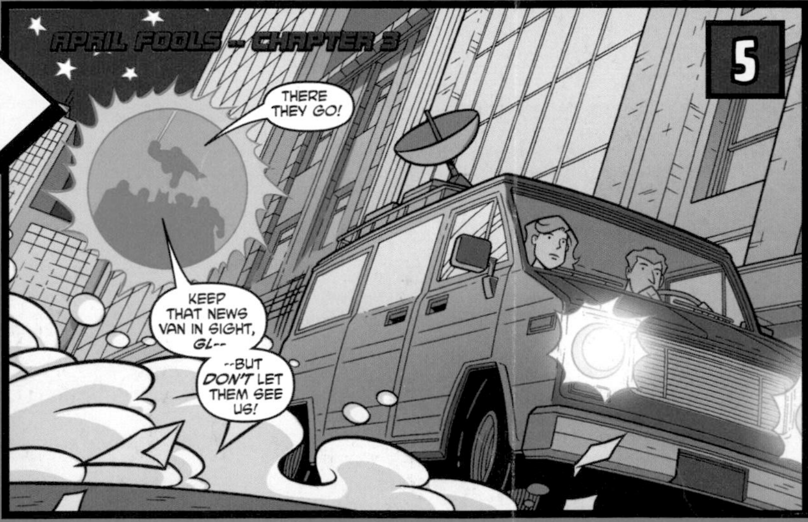

APRIL FOOLS -- CHAPTER 3
5
THERE THEY GO!
KEEP THAT NEWS VAN IN SIGHT, GL--
--BUT DON'T LET THEM SEE US!

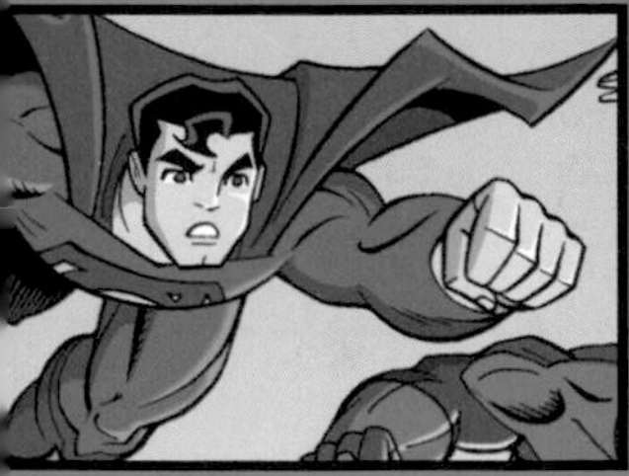

6. What practical jokes are the Jester's League members preparing? What other practical jokes could they have pulled?

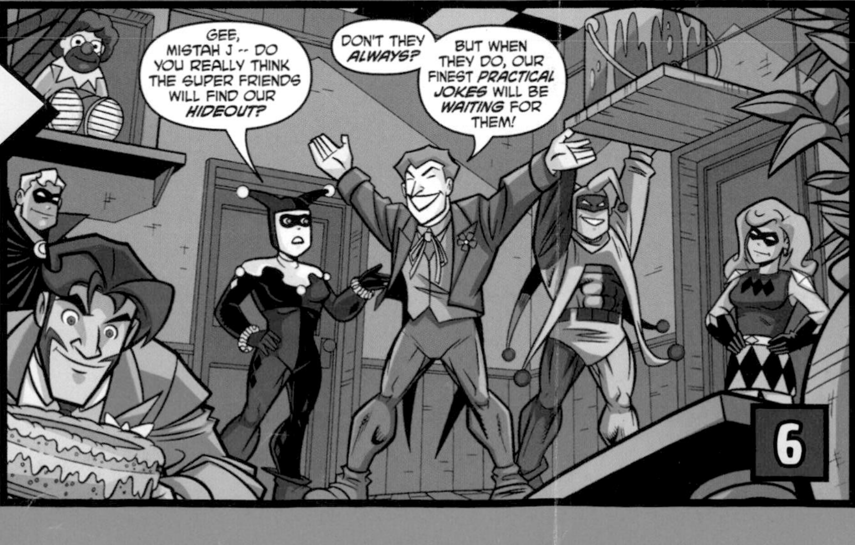

GEE, MISTAH J -- DO YOU REALLY THINK THE SUPER FRIENDS WILL FIND OUR HIDEOUT?
DON'T THEY ALWAYS?
BUT WHEN THEY DO, OUR FINEST PRACTICAL JOKES WILL BE WAITING FOR THEM!
6

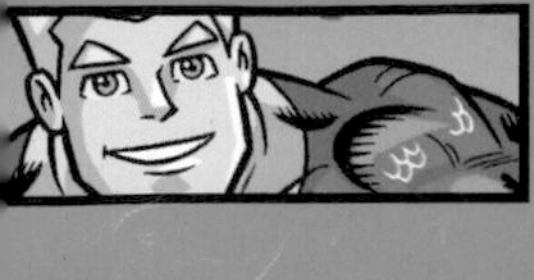

READ THEM ALL!

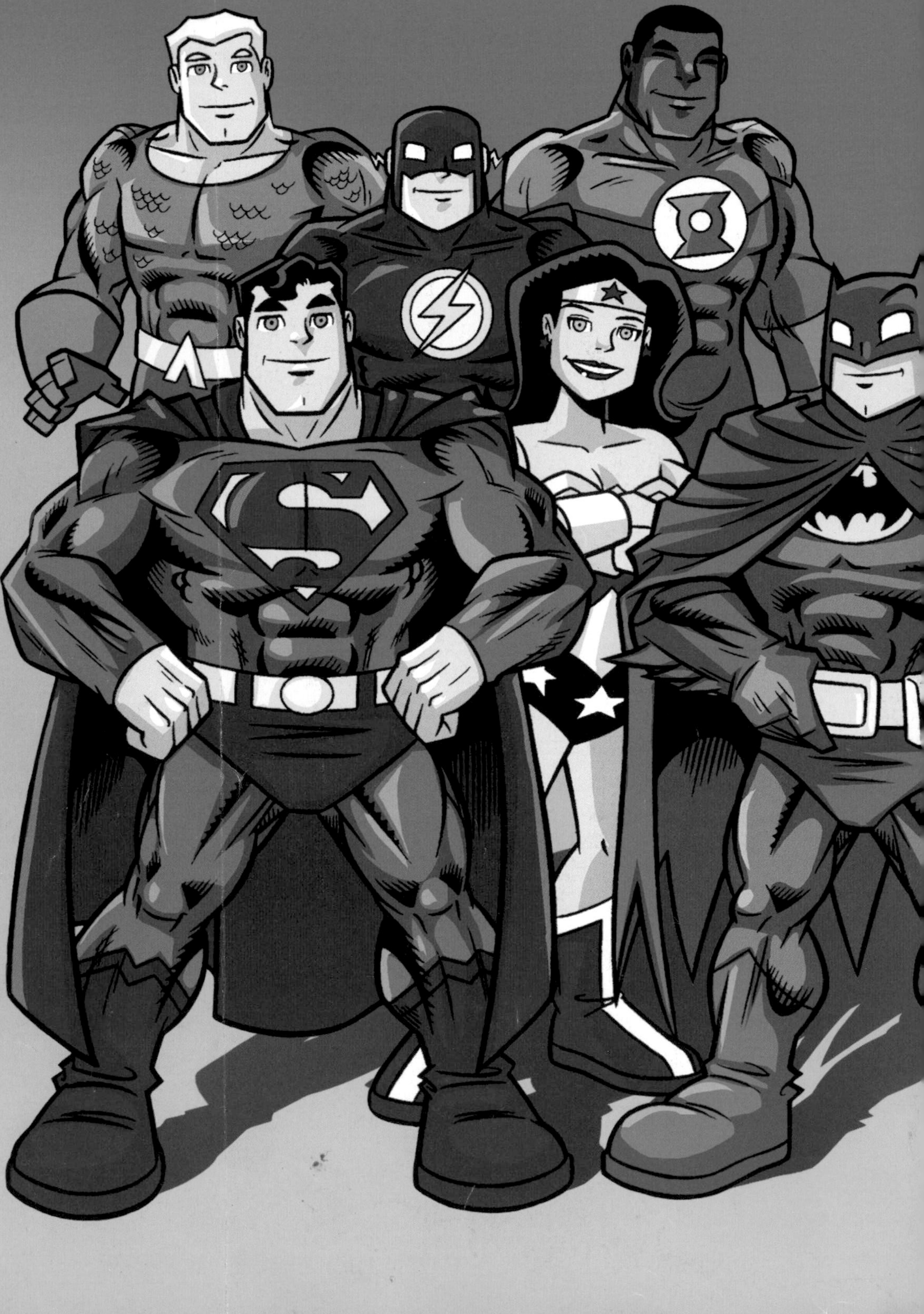

DC SUPER FRIENDS™

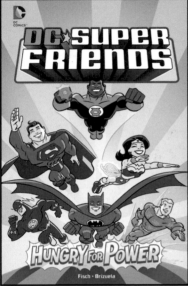

DC COMICS
DC SUPER FRIENDS
HUNGRY FOR POWER
Fisch • Brizuela
Hungry for Power

DC COMICS
DC SUPER FRIENDS
DINOSAUR ROUND-UP
Fisch • Ottolini • Staton
Dinosaur Round-up

DC COMICS
DC SUPER FRIENDS
WANTED: THE SUPER FRIENDS
Fisch • McKenny • Moy
Wanted: The Super Friends

DC COMICS
DC SUPER FRIENDS
APRIL FOOLS
Fisch • Brizuela
April Fools

ONLY FROM...

STONE ARCH BOOKS™
a capstone imprint www.capstonepub.com

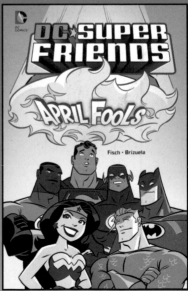

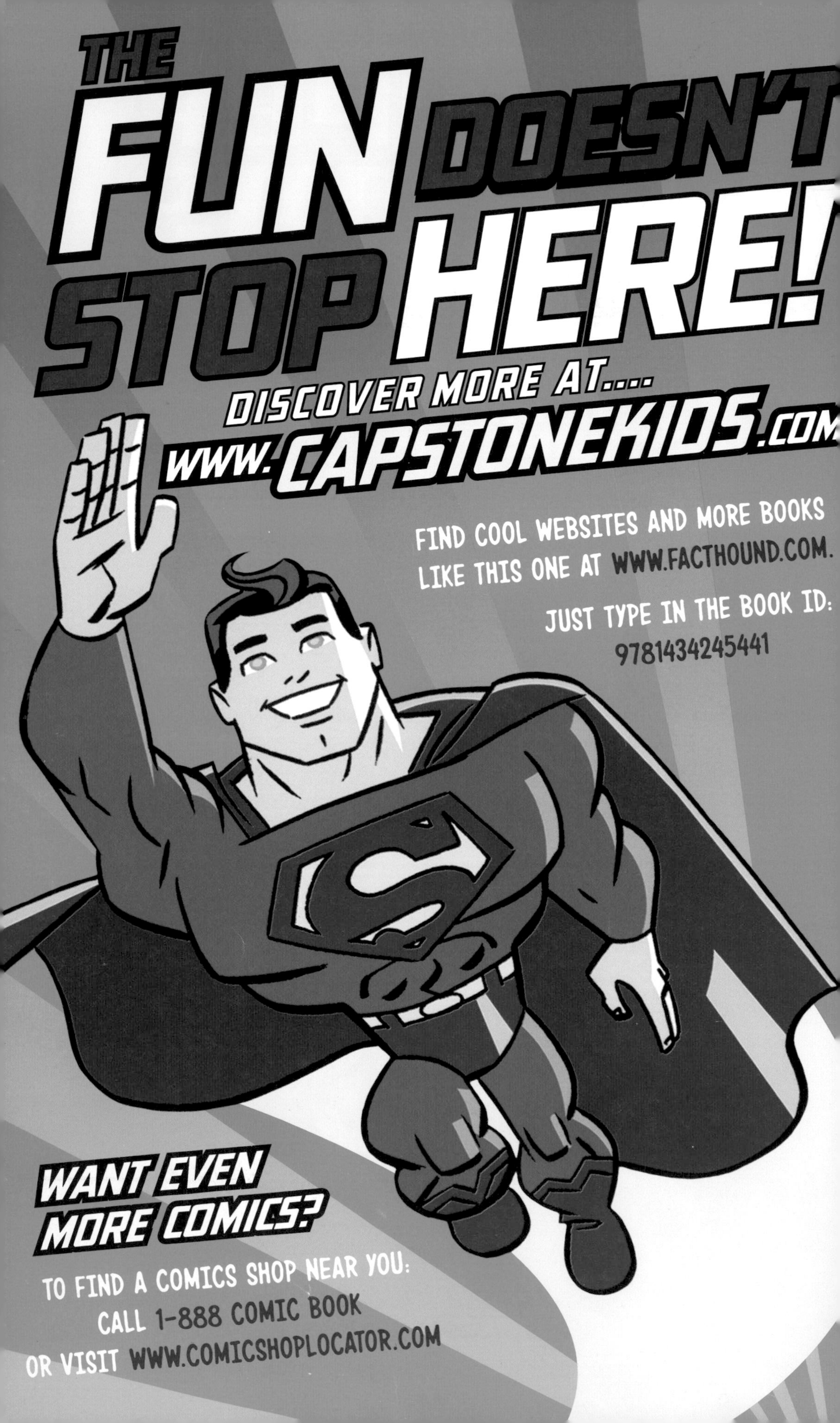
THE FUN DOESN'T STOP HERE!
DISCOVER MORE AT....
WWW.CAPSTONEKIDS.COM
FIND COOL WEBSITES AND MORE BOOKS LIKE THIS ONE AT WWW.FACTHOUND.COM.
JUST TYPE IN THE BOOK ID:
9781434245441
WANT EVEN MORE COMICS?
TO FIND A COMICS SHOP NEAR YOU:
CALL 1-888 COMIC BOOK
OR VISIT WWW.COMICSHOPLOCATOR.COM